喚醒你的英文語感！

Get a Feel for English !

喚醒你的英文語感！

Get a Feel for English !

從聽不懂到流利對談的學習奇蹟！

職場英文進化術

作者：商英教父 Quentin Brand

Listening • Speaking

基礎篇

Upgrade Your Biz English

貝塔語言出版
Beta Multimedia Publishing

IRT 語言測驗中心
Language Testing Center

目錄 CONTENTS

Part 4 簡報篇 Presentation

Unit 1

前言

英文聽不懂？！事出必有因

大部分英文學者都會同意聽英文是一件困難的事。無論你是聽收音機或看電視，聽其他人的交談、或對你說的話，要完全聽懂並不容易。聽比讀、說或寫都需要更大程度的專注力。不過，好的聽力在商業場合和日常生活都是相當重要的。羅馬歷史學家蒲魯塔克（Plutarch）說：Know how to listen, and you will profit even from those who talk badly.「知道如何傾聽，你甚至也能從無法清楚表達的那些人身上獲益。」好的聽力不僅是專心聽人們說些什麼，還要聽他們怎麼說。

這套書希望能幫助各位加強英文聽力和口說。我們先思考下一個問題。

動動腦 請想想，聽英文對你之所以困難的原因。

分析

以下是一些最常見的原因。哪一項你也心有戚戚焉呢？

- **速度**：講話者（尤其是母語人士）說得太快。
- **口音**：口音可以聽出你是哪裡人。有些人的口音和其他人相當不一樣，所以我可能是不熟悉他的口音。
- **發音**：發音指的是每個人對某些音（sound）的發聲方式。非母語人士對某些音可能有自己的發聲方式，我需要花一點時間才能適應。
- **字彙**：我可能沒有足夠的字彙量來了解討論的主題。
- **俚語**：母語人士說話尤其會使用許多我不懂的俚語。
- **其他**：也許對話是在吵雜的環境進行，或者你在使用的電話收訊不清楚，又或者是對方的聲音太小。

以上原因都可能造成聽力障礙。很遺憾，並沒有簡單的解決之道。沒有神奇之鑰可以讓你轉動，然後突然間你就可以完全聽懂英文。不過，還是有一些技巧可以幫助你加強聽力。這套書會教你這些技巧，方法就是讓你對於口說英文的特徵有更強的敏銳度。有了敏銳度自然就能提升聽力。

第一本「基礎篇」是針對使用英文做生意的商業情境。第二本「菁英篇」則著重在使用英文談論各種商業議題。

口音種類比你想的還要多

先前討論的聽力障礙之一是口音。口音可以聽出你是哪裡人，而英語有很多不同的口音，包括非母語人士和母語人士。

動動腦 請看看下方的圖表。

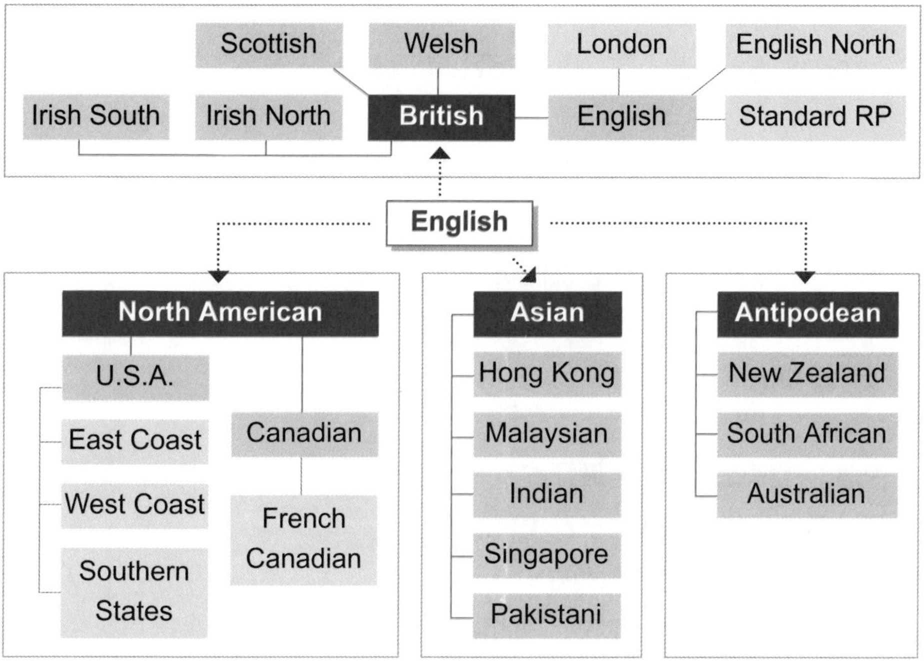

分析

這個圖表顯示出英語口音的多樣性。你可以看到有四個主要族群：英國（British）、北美（North American）、亞洲（Asian）和另一個半球（Antipodean）。

- 英式英語包含許多不同的口音，看你是來自倫敦、英國北方、蘇格蘭、愛爾蘭或威爾斯。即使是愛爾蘭南方和愛爾蘭北方的口音也很不同。我本身說的是標準發音，是英國南方的口音。當你收聽 BBC 新聞時，聽到的就是這種口音。
- 北美英文包含加拿大和美國英文，兩者很不同。在美國境內也有很多不同的口音，德克薩斯州人和紐約人說話就很不一樣。
- 另一個半球的口音彼此也很不同，南非人和澳洲人說話就很不一樣。
- 在亞洲以英語為母語的國家（通常是不列顛帝國以前的殖民地）也有很不一樣的各種口音。例如，在印度，英文是政府的官方語言，很多印度人和巴基斯坦人都認為他們自己是英語母語人士，不過他們的發音和其他任何英語系國家都相當不同。馬來西亞和新加坡也是一樣。

當然，還有好幾百種不一樣的非英語系英語，那些就沒有列在上一頁的圖表中了。

所以，你要拿這各式各樣的英文口音怎麼辦？也許你會想，我要怎麼學會每一種？當然囉，這是不可能的任務。不過，關於所有的這些英文，有幾件重要的事必須記住。

1. 中庸的標準母語英文是最好的。
2. 每一種母語英文都有它自己獨特的發音。
3. 每一種母語英文都是正確的。
4. 其實，各種母語英文都有共同的口說特色，這部分容我稍後再述。

5. 很多時候，即使是母語人士也無法彼此互相了解。例如，我自己就很難了解格拉斯哥（蘇格蘭西岸的一個城市）的人說些什麼。
6. 其實，你在面對不同的英語人士（英語系或非英語系）時所遇到的聽力障礙，也正是他們要聽懂你說什麼時所面臨的困難。

最後一點很重要。切記，別人要聽懂你就如同你要聽懂他們有著一樣的困難。這可能會讓你覺得好過一點。保持耐心，如果聽不懂，請對方重述一次；反之，如果你覺得對方無法理解你說些什麼，就把事情慢慢再講一次。這有助於雙方的溝通。

口說英文的特色就這些

現在讓我們來看看英文口說的共同特色。無論母語人士是哪裡人，或他說的是哪一種英文，英文口說都有幾個共同特色，非常重要。認識這些共同特色有助於你聽懂英文。

在口說中，字 (words) 絕對不會單獨使用。字會和其他字一起出現，這在下列四個方面影響了英語的發音。

❶ 連音

連音就是說話時把字連在一起的現象，尤其是話說得很快時。

例句

母語人士不會說： I'm interested in tennis.

他們會說： I'm interested in tennis.

把 I'm 和 interested 連在一起、再把 interested 和 in 連在一起。前一個字會和下一個字連在一起，發音一氣呵成，而不會每個字都唸得很清楚。

要聽出連在一起的字有哪些，需要時間練習。

❷ 弱化音

在句子裡有一些字會比其他字來得重要。一般而言，「內容」或「意義字」比「文法」或「功能字」更爲重要。舉例來說，在下面這個句子：I was walking along the street when I saw my pal Bob. 當中，I 、 walking 、 street 、 saw 、 Bob 都是內容字，其他的則是功能字。大多時候，功能字的發音都非常急促，它們的母音通常會有變化，字的聲音好像被說話者吞下去一樣。這些就稱爲弱化音。非母語人士在聆聽時，常搞不清楚這些功能字的弱化音，尤其是當它們和重要的意義字連在一起的時候。如果你試圖要聽懂每一個單獨的字，只會徒增聽力障礙。

❸ 句子重音

連音和弱化音加在一起就產生了句子的韻律。韻律是由意義字所主導，每一個句子都有它自己的韻律，稱爲句子重音。如果你了解句子重音如何運作，那麼你要聽懂流暢的口說英文就更容易了。

❹ 語調

除了句子重音，語調也是口說英文很重要的一部分。語調就是聲音的旋律，有時候你說話聲音會上揚，有時候聲音會下降。句子裡的重音字「通常」都會用比較高的語調，但也可能不是。語調不只能幫助你理解說話者在說什麼，還能聽出他的情緒。如果你了解語調如何運作，那麼你要用英文有效溝通就更容易了。

如何使用本書

本書將提升你對於口說英文特徵的敏銳度，並幫助你聽懂它們。

語言學習是有趣的一件事，如果你改善發音，聽力會跟著進步；反之，如果你專注於聽力，發音也會跟著進步。這是一個良性循環，也是我們在本書將採取的模式。你將會「聽到」很多包含上述特徵的「口說」範例。

第一部分　此部分的重點是社交英文，以及上述四項口說特徵在社交英文的使用情形。

第二部分　重點是開會時的聽力障礙，尤其是語調的使用。

第三部分　重點是電話英文的聽力。你將會聽到許多電話對談，並練習理解當中的重要訊息。

第四部分　重點是英文簡報的聽力。你將會練習如何聽取關鍵資訊。

你可以將本書從頭至尾逐章讀完，也可以根據你最急迫的需求，挑選其中的章節來研讀。無論你選擇哪一種方式閱讀本書，我都必須再次強調，確實按照書中的指示來聽英文是非常重要的，唯有如此，你的聽力才會眞正地提升！

祝你聆聽愉快！

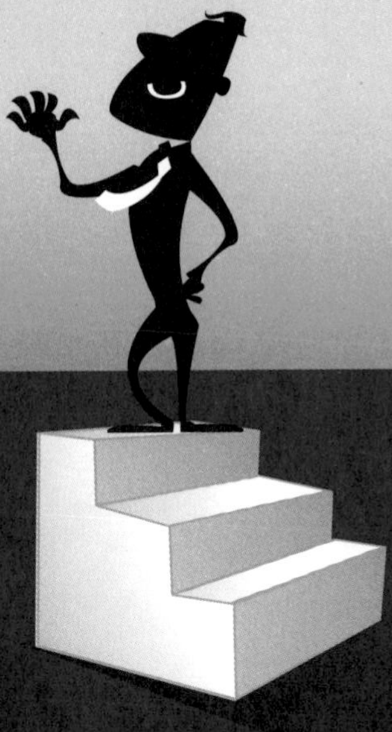

Part 1

社交篇

Socializing

Unit 2

What Are You Up to Later?

你待會兒要做什麼？

學習重點 纏著左鄰右舍的助動詞

聽聽看

1 Paul 和 Mary 在員工聚會上相遇。請聽聽他們之間的對話，你能夠聽懂哪些事情呢？接著再聽第二次，這一次請專心聽 Paul 和 Mary 詢問彼此的問題。 Track 002

英文的問句有點複雜。它們的文法難懂，而且有時候很難正確地聽出來。問句意義的表達關鍵就在助動詞，共有五種。

動動腦

2 請讀一讀下列表格，確定你了解之後再繼續往下閱讀。

助動詞	範例	意義
are/is do/does have/has	Are you having a good time? Where do you come from? Have you been here long?	表達現在時間或無關時間
were/was did	How was it? Where did you go?	表達過去時間

分析

- Are/is、do/does 和 have/has 通常用來表示關於現在時間、事實或選擇的問句，或是關於現在的情境。Did 和 were/was 則用在關於過去動作或狀態的問句中。
- 請記得，are、have 和 were 是用在主詞為 you 或 they 的問句；is、does、has 和 was 則是用在主詞為 he、she 或 it 的句子；did 可以適用於所有主詞。

在一般談話中，助動詞通常比較難被清楚聽到，但它們卻很重要，因爲如果你誤解它們，就無法掌握問句要表達的時間。

助動詞都是非重讀字，經常會和前面或後面的字連結。

動動腦 3 請看看下列句子，在口說中通常會怎麼唸。

- How are you?
  → **How are you?**
- Are you having a good time?
  → **Are you HAVING a good time?**
- Where do you come from?
  → **Where do you COME from?**
- Do you do any sports?
  → **Do you DO any sports?**
- What does your wife do?
  → **What does your wife DO?**
- Does she like it here?
  → **Does she LIKE it here?**
- Have you been here long?
  → **Have you BEEN here long?**
- Have you eaten this kind of food before?
  → **Have you EATEN this kind of food before?**
- Has she found a job yet?
  → **Has she FOUND a job yet?**

• Has he made any friends?

→ **Has he MADE any friends?**

• Where did you go?

→ **Where did you GO?**

• Where did you get your car?

→ **Where did you GET your car?**

• Were there many people?

→ **Were there many people?**

分 析

注意，句子中的主要動詞永遠都需要重讀（如上列句子中的大寫字）；助動詞則通常與後面的字連結，而有省略音素 (elided) 的情形。

事實上，發音規則相當複雜，要聽出助動詞的最佳方法就是練習唸例句。我們就從發音訓練開始，這樣你要聽出字串就更容易了。

說說看

4 跟著 CD 來練習這些口說字串。儘量說快一點，就像 CD 上的唸法一樣。 Track 003

1. **… are you …**

2. **… do you …**

3. **… have you …**

4. **… were you …**

5. ... did you ...

6. ... is he ...

7. ... is she ...

8. ... is it ...

9. ... does he ...

10. ... does she ...

11. ... does it ...

12. ... has he ...

13. ... has she ...

14. ... has it ...

15. ... was it ...

16. ... did it ...

熟唸之後，接著來看看你是否可以在問句中聽出這些字串。

聽聽看

5 請仔細聽問句，並選出你所聽到的字串。請看範例。

Track 004

a	1.	a) ... are you ...	b) ... do you ...
____	2.	a) ... did it ...	b) ... did you ...
____	3.	a) ... were you ...	b) ... are you ...
____	4.	a) ... did you ...	b) ... did he ...
____	5.	a) ... does he ...	b) ... do you ...
____	6.	a) ... does he ...	b) ... does she ...
____	7.	a) ... has he ...	b) ... have you ...
____	8.	a) ... did it ...	b) ... does it ...
____	9.	a) ... has he ...	b) ... is he ...

______ **10.** a) … are you … b) … do you …

______ **11.** a) … have you … b) … has he …

______ **12.** a) … is she … b) … has she …

______ **13.** a) … are you … b) … have you …

______ **14.** a) … is it … b) … is he …

______ **15.** a) … was it … b) … has it …

______ **16.** a) … does he … b) … did you …

______ **17.** a) … are you … b) … did you …

______ **18.** a) … is it … b) … has it …

______ **19.** a) … are you … b) … do you …

______ **20.** a) … was it … b) … has he …

______ **21.** a) … have you … b) … has he …

______ **22.** a) … have you … b) … are you …

______ **23.** a) … do you … b) … does he …

______ **24.** a) … is he … b) … has he …

______ **25.** a) … was it … b) … is it …

答案 請見29頁。

如果第一次無法完全聽懂，可以多聽幾次。

聽聽看

6 請選出你所聽到的問句。

Track 005

______ **1.** a) Where are you from?

b) Where was it from?

_______ **2.** a) Did he have any children?

b) Do you have any children?

_______ **3.** a) Have you been to Kaohsiung?

b) Are you going to Kaohsiung?

_______ **4.** a) What were you doing?

b) Where are you going?

_______ **5.** a) Do you see Jon?

b) Did you see Jon?

_______ **6.** a) Is he happy here?

b) Is she happy here?

_______ **7.** a) Is she easy to get along with?

b) Is he easygoing?

_______ **8.** a) How far was it?

b) What time is it?

_______ **9.** a) What does he do?

b) What is he wearing?

_______ **10.** a) Where does she live?

b) Where is she living?

_______ **11.** a) What does he mean?

b) What does it mean?

_______ **12.** a) Has he been here before?

b) Is he coming again?

_______ **13.** a) Has she made any friends?

b) Is she making friends?

_______ **14.** a) Has it always been like this?

b) What is it like?

_______ **15.** a) Is it difficult to find?

b) Was it difficult to find?

_______ **16.** a) Did it go well?

b) Does it go well?

答案 請見29頁。

在聽下一段對話之前，請回頭復習一下先前所學的對話和口說技巧，不要忘了利用CD來輔助你。如果能夠掌握先前所學的要點，你會發現，要聽懂下一段對話並不是困難的事喔。

聽聽看

7 現在請聽另一段對話，聽的時候，請專注於你在本章所學到的重點，看看你進步了多少？ Track 006

解答

聽聽看 5

1. a	2. b	3. b	4. a	5. b
6. a	7. b	8. b	9. a	10. b
11. a	12. b	13. b	14. a	15. a
16. b	17. a	18. a	19. b	20. b
21. a	22. b	23. a	24. b	25. a

聽聽看 6

1. a	2. b	3. a	4. a	5. b	
6. a	7. a	8. b	9. a	10. a	
11. b	12. a	13. a	14. a	15. b	16. a

CD 內容

Track 002

Mary: Hi! How are you?

Paul: I'm good, thanks. How are you?

Mary: Well, I'm good too, I guess. Are you having a good time?

Paul: Yes. It's nice to meet all these new people. You know I just arrived here, so everything is kind of new for me.

Mary: Oh, right, yes. You're the new guy. Welcome!

Paul: Thanks!

Mary: So, where do you come from?

Paul: I'm from the States, from Washington.

Mary: Wow. Have you been here long?

Paul: Well, I arrived about three weeks ago with my family, and we've been settling in.

Mary: You brought your family? Wow! What does your wife do?

Paul: Well, she's just at home taking care of our son.

Mary: I see. And does she like it here?

Paul: Yes, she's making new friends and getting to know the neighbors.

Mary: Has she found a job yet?

Paul: No, she's not going to work.

Mary: And your son, has he made any friends? I have two kids, ten and eleven. Maybe we could get them together.

Paul: Well, my son is fifteen, so he might find your kids too young! But thanks anyway.

Mary: Sure. So do you do any sports?

Paul: Yes, I like tennis. You?

Mary: Mmm. Golf is more my thing.

Paul: Oh. Golf is good.

Mary: Have you eaten this kind of food before?

Paul: No, it's kind of strange. What is it?

Mary: It's frog, actually.

Paul: Tastes really good. Hey look, maybe you can help me. I need to buy a car. Where did you get your car?

Mary: Well, it's a company car. I'm sure they'll give you one, too.

Paul: I hope so. I want to go on some excursions on the weekends, you know, have a look around the place.

Mary: Oh, yes, we take lots of trips on the weekends. We had a great time last weekend.

Paul: Really? Where did you go?

Mary: We went to a place called Wulai.

Paul: Oh, yes, I know that place. How was it?

Mary: Oh, it was great. The kids swam in the river.

Paul: Were there many people?

Mary: Not really. It was peaceful.

【中譯】

Mary: 嗨，你好嗎？

Paul: 很好，謝謝。妳呢？

Mary: 喔，我也很好，算是吧。你開心嗎？

Paul: 是啊，很高興能和這些新面孔見面。妳知道我剛到這裡，所以每件事對我來說都還挺新鮮的。

Mary: 喔，對，你就是新來的人。歡迎你！

Paul: 謝謝！

Mary: 那，你是哪裡人？

Paul: 我是美國人，來自華盛頓州。

Mary: 哇，你來很久了嗎？

Paul: 我大約是三個星期前和我的家人來到這裡，我們已經安頓下來了。

Mary: 你帶你的家人來？哇！你太太是做什麼的？

Paul: 她只是在家裡照顧我們的兒子。

Mary: 這樣啊。那她喜歡這裡嗎？

Paul: 是啊，她正在交新朋友和認識鄰居呢。

Mary: 她找到工作了嗎？

Paul: 沒有，她不打算工作。

Mary: 那你兒子呢？他已經交到任何朋友了嗎？我有兩個孩子，十歲和十一歲。也許我們可以讓他們見見面。

Paul: 呃，我兒子十五歲，所以他可能會覺得妳孩子太小了！不過還是很謝謝妳。

Mary: 沒什麼。那麼你有做任何運動嗎？

Paul: 有，我喜歡網球。妳呢？

Mary: 嗯……我比較喜歡高爾夫球。

Paul: 哦，高爾夫球不錯啊。

Mary: 你以前有吃過這類食物嗎？

Paul: 沒有，這有點奇怪。這是什麼？

Mary: 事實上，這是青蛙。

Paul: 真的很好吃。啊，對了，也許妳可以幫我一個忙，我需要買部車，妳的車是在哪裡買的？

Mary: 是公司車。我相信他們也會給你一部的。

Paul: 我希望是這樣。我想在週末時出去逛一逛，妳知道的，看看這個地方。

Mary: 是啊，我們常在週末出去。上週末我們就玩得很愉快。

Paul: 真的嗎？妳們去哪裡？

Mary: 我們去了一個叫做烏來的地方。

Paul: 是喔，我知道那個地方。那地方怎麼樣？

Mary: 喔，那地方很棒。孩子們在河裡游泳。

Paul: 有很多遊客嗎？

Mary: 沒有，那地方很寧靜。

Track 004

1. Are you enjoying living here?
2. Did you go out this weekend?
3. Are you planning on staying long?
4. Did you have a good time?
5. Do you like it here?
6. Does he like his school?
7. What other countries have you visited?
8. Does it rain often in your country?
9. Has he told you about the new project?
10. Do you miss home?
11. Have you seen the new Batman movie yet?
12. What has she been doing while you're away?
13. What have you been doing since I saw you last?
14. Is it easy to get a job in your country?
15. Was it cold?
16. What did you do this weekend?
17. Where are you living at the moment?
18. Is it hot in your country?
19. What do you want to do later?

20. What has he been doing over the long vacation?

21. What other movies have you seen recently?

22. Where are you from?

23. Where do you live?

24. Where has he been?

25. Where was it made?

【中譯】

1. 你喜歡住在這裡嗎？
2. 你這週末有外出嗎？
3. 你打算待很久嗎？
4. 你玩得愉快嗎？
5. 你喜歡這裡嗎？
6. 他喜歡他的學校嗎？
7. 你造訪過其他哪些國家？
8. 在你們國家經常下雨嗎？
9. 他告訴你新專案的事了嗎？
10. 你想家嗎？
11. 你看過新的蝙蝠俠電影沒？
12. 你不在時她都做了些什麼？
13. 自從我們上次碰面之後你都在做些什麼？
14. 在你們國家找工作容易嗎？
15. 天氣冷嗎？
16. 你這個週末做了什麼？
17. 你目前住在哪裡？
18. 你們國家天氣熱嗎？
19. 你等一下想做什麼？

20. 這麼長的假期他都做了些什麼？
21. 你最近看過哪些電影？
22. 你是哪裡人？
23. 你住哪裡？
24. 他去哪裡了？
25. 它是哪裡製造的？

Track 005

1. Where are you from?
2. Do you have any children?
3. Have you been to Kaohsiung?
4. What were you doing?
5. Did you see John?
6. Is he happy here?
7. Is she easy to get along with?
8. What time is it?
9. What does he do?
10. Where does she live?
11. What does it mean?
12. Has he been here before?
13. Has she made any friends?
14. Has it always been like this?
15. Was it difficult to find?
16. Did it go well?

【中譯】

1. 你是哪裡人？

2. 你有孩子嗎？
3. 你去過高雄嗎？
4. 你（那時）在做什麼？
5. 你有見到約翰嗎？
6. 他在這裡快樂嗎？
7. 她容易相處嗎？
8. 現在幾點鐘？
9. 他從事什麼工作？
10. 她住哪裡？
11. 那是什麼意思？
12. 他以前來過這裡嗎？
13. 她已經交到任何朋友了嗎？
14. （天氣）一直都是像這樣嗎？
15. 很難找得到嗎？
16. 進行得順利嗎？

Track 006

Julie: Hi.

Frank: Hello.

Julie: What's your name?

Frank: Frank. What's yours?

Julie: Julie.

Frank: Nice to meet you.

Julie: Nice to meet you too, Frank. Where are you from?

Frank: Oh, I'm from England.

Julie: England! Oh, wow. So have you been living in Taiwan long?

Frank: About six months.

Julie: So what are you doing here, if you don't mind my asking?

Frank: Ha ha. Well, I was transferred here by my company.

Julie: I see. Where were you working before?

Frank: Before, I was in Russia.

Julie: Oh, really! Was it cold there?

Frank: Ha ha ha! Very! Too cold. We asked to be transferred somewhere warmer, so they gave us Taipei.

Julie: Cool! And do you like it here?

Frank: So far, yes, it's pretty nice, and the people are quite friendly.

Julie: Yes, we like foreigners. Did it take you long to get used to it? I mean was it difficult to settle down?

Frank: No, not really, we both settled down quite fast.

Julie: Do you have your family here with you?

Frank: My wife.

Julie: So you're married. Mmm. How long have you been married?

Frank: About ten years.

Julie: Oh, so long! Congratulations. Does your wife have a job here as well?

Frank: Yes. She works for an international company here as well.

Julie: Oh, right. Did she also get transferred?

Frank: Yes. Luckily! Otherwise one of us would have had to have found a new job. What about you? Does your husband work in Taipei?

Julie: No, he works in Hong Kong, and I work here.

Frank: Oh, I see. Is it difficult for you to live apart like that?

Julie: Well, he comes back every weekend, so I guess it's OK.

Frank: Has he got a good job there?

Julie: Oh yes, otherwise we wouldn't live like this.

Frank: Is it difficult to find a job in Hong Kong? I mean, why don't you both live there?

Julie: I have to look after my father here in Taiwan.

Frank: Oh, right.

Julie: My mother died about ten years ago, and we have no other family, so I have to look after him. Anyway, you got kids?

Frank: No.

Julie: Were you thinking of having any?

Frank: Not right now ….

【中譯】

Julie: 嗨。

Frank: 哈囉。

Julie: 你叫什麼名字？

Frank: Frank，妳呢？

Julie: Julie。

Frank: 很高興認識妳。

Julie: 我也很高興認識你，Frank。你是哪裡人？

Frank: 哦，我是英國人。

Julie: 英國！喔，哇。那你已經在台灣住很久了嗎？

Frank: 六個月左右。

Julie: 你在這裡從事什麼工作，你不介意我這麼問吧？

Frank: 哈哈。呃，我是被公司調到這裡的。

Julie: 這樣啊。你之前在哪裡工作？

Frank: 以前，我在蘇俄。

Julie: 哦，真的啊！那裡天氣冷嗎？

Frank: 哈哈哈！非常冷！太冷囉！我們要求調到比較溫暖的國家，所以他們就派我們到台北來了。

Julie: 酷！那你喜歡這裡嗎？

Frank: 到目前為止，是的，這地方挺不賴的，人們也相當友善。

Julie: 是啊，我們喜歡外國人。你有花很長時間來適應嗎？我是說穩定下來很難嗎？

Frank: 不，不算難，我們兩個人都很快就穩定下來了。

Julie: 你和你的家人一起來的嗎？

Frank: 我太太。

Julie: 所以你結婚了。嗯……你結婚多久了？

Frank: 大概十年。

Julie: 哦，這麼久了！恭喜啊。你太太在這裡也有工作嗎？

Frank: 是的。她在這裡也是服務於一家跨國公司。

Julie: 哦，是喔。她也是被調派的嗎？

Frank: 是啊，真幸運！要不然我們其中一個人就得找新工作了。那妳呢？妳先生也在台北工作嗎？

Julie: 不，他在香港工作，而我在這裡工作。

Frank: 哦，這樣啊。像這樣分開住對你們來說有困難嗎？

Julie: 呃，他每個週末都會回來，所以我想是還好啦。

Frank: 他在那裡找到了一份好工作嗎？

Julie: 哦，對啊，要不然我們就不會像這樣分開住了。

Frank: 在香港找工作困難嗎？我是說，你們為什麼不兩個人都住那裡呢？

Julie: 我必須在台灣照顧我爸爸。

Frank: 哦，是喔。

Julie: 我媽媽十年前過世了，我們沒有其他的家人，所以我必須照顧他。反正就這樣啦，你有孩子嗎？

Frank: 沒有。

Julie: 你有想過要生嗎？

Frank: 還不是時候……

Unit 3

Anything You Can Do, I Can Do Better.

所有你做的，我都可以做更好！

學習重點 can、can't 傻傻分不清楚

聽聽看

1 現在是下午休息時間 (coffee break)。請聽 Janice 和 Peter 的對話，你能夠聽出哪些事情呢？接著再聽一遍，這次請試著完成下列表格，他們精通哪些語言呢？

Track 007

	Janice	Peter
can	speak French	
can't		

答案 請見48頁。

「can」和「can't」的發音有時候很難分辨。事實上，這兩個字在英式英語和美式英語的說法是有差異的。

美式英語

■ Can 在肯定句的發音是 /kæn/，在問句也是。

■ Can't 的發音是 /kænt/。/kæn/ 和 /kænt/ 都是重讀字。如：I CAN SPEAK ...、I CAN'T SPEAK ...、CAN you SPEAK …?

■ 肯定與否定之間的差異就在否定字的尾音 /t/，你必須留意是否有 /t/ 這個音。

英式英語

■ Can 在肯定句和問句中的發音是 /kən/，不是重讀字。重音落在下一個動詞。如：I can SPEAK ...。

■ Can't 的發音近似 /kɑnt/，是重讀字。這表示在否定句中你會聽到兩個連續的重讀字。如： I CAN'T SPEAK ...。

■ 很多時候， can't 的尾音 /t/ 是不發音的，所以你必須留意字的重音模式。

■ 如果 can 後面沒有字，那麼它就要重讀，發音方式類似美式英語的 can 。如： Yes, I CAN.。

聽聽看

2 下列表格為美式和英式英語的差異摘要。請復習並聽 CD 的示範。 Track 008

	肯定	否定	問句	單獨
美式發音	/kæn/	/kænt/	/kæn/	/kæn/
英式發音	/kæn/	/kɑnt/	/kæn/	/kæn/

爲了讓各位更熟悉這些發音的差異，我們接著來聽更多的例句吧。首先來聽美式英語的範例。

聽聽看

3 請聽這些句子，它們各是肯定還是否定句呢？請在正確的欄位打勾。 Track 009

	肯定	否定
1.	( )	( )
2.	( )	( )
3.	( )	( )
4.	( )	( )
5.	( )	( )
6.	( )	( )

7.	(　　)	(　　)
8.	(　　)	(　　)
9.	(　　)	(　　)
10.	(　　)	(　　)
11.	(　　)	(　　)
12.	(　　)	(　　)

答案 請參見51頁的CD內容。

第一次聽也許會覺得很難，不要擔心，熟聽幾次後，自然就能夠分辨can和can't之間的發音差異。接著我們用同樣的方式來練習英式英語的部分。

聽聽看

4 請聽這些句子，它們各是肯定還是否定句呢？請在正確的欄位打勾。 Track 010

	肯定	否定
1.	(　　)	(　　)
2.	(　　)	(　　)
3.	(　　)	(　　)
4.	(　　)	(　　)
5.	(　　)	(　　)
6.	(　　)	(　　)
7.	(　　)	(　　)
8.	(　　)	(　　)
9.	(　　)	(　　)
10.	(　　)	(　　)

11. (   )   (   )

12. (   )   (   )

答案 請參見52頁的CD內容。

歷經can和can't的聽力密集訓練，現在是不是更有把握，不會再傻傻分不清楚can 和 can't呢？！可以再回頭聽聽Janice和Peter的對話，相信先前的盲點，這次都可以聽懂了。

切記，要提升你對於口說英文特徵的敏銳度，最好的方法就是學會如何使用它們。

說說看

5
- 列出一些你能做的事情，和你不能做的事情。
- 練習把這些事情說出來，就像先前聽力練習中的句子一樣。
- 如果可以找到同伴一起練習，請聽對方說出的句子，並判斷是肯定句或否定句。

接著我們來學習一些含有 can 和 can't 的常用俚語。

聽聽看

6 **請聽 CD 中的俚語，並以 can 或 can't 完成填空。**

Track 011

1. You ________ talk!

2. If you ________ beat 'em, join 'em.

3. ________ win 'em all.

4. You ________ say that again!

5. I ________ believe my ears!

6. Do it as best you ________.

7. ________ hear myself think.

8. Nice work if you ________ get it.

9. You ________ bet your bottom dollar.

10. ________ be bothered.

答案 請見48頁。

聽出這些俚語使用的是 can 或 can't 之後，你知道它們的意思爲何嗎？接著我們就來揭曉答案吧。

動動腦 7 請將下列俚語與它們所代表的意思配對。

_____ **1.** You can talk!

_____ **2.** If you can't beat 'em, join 'em.

_____ **3.** Can't win 'em all.

_____ **4.** You can say that again!

_____ **5.** I can't believe my ears!

_____ **6.** Do it as best you can.

_____ **7.** Can't hear myself think.

_____ **8.** Nice work if you can get it.

_____ **9.** You can bet your bottom dollar.

_____ **10.** Can't be bothered.

a) Do something to the best of your ability.

b) I am completely certain that something will happen.

c) I don't believe what you're telling me!

d) I don't want to make the effort to do it.

e) It's an easy way to earn money, but you need to be lucky as well.

f) It's so noisy in here!

g) It's not possible to succeed every time.

h) Other people are doing something bad, and I can't stop them so I will do it too!

i) Don't criticize me for doing something, when you also do it yourself!

j) You're absolutely right!

答案 請見48頁。

請回頭再聽一遍Peter和Janice的對談，他們用了多少個俚語呢？相信這一次，你應該能聽懂和理解更多。

聽聽看

8 現在請聽另一段對話，聽的時候專注在本章所學的重點，看看你進步了多少？ Track 012

解答

聽聽看 1

	Janice	Peter
can	speak French speak German speak Chinese	speak Japanese speak English speak Chinese read Chinese
can't	speak Japanese read and write Chinese	speak European languages

聽聽看 6

1. can 2. can't 3. Can't
4. can 5. can't 6. can
7. Can't 8. can 9. can 10. Can't

動動腦 7

1. i 2. h 3. g 4. j 5. c
6. a 7. f 8. e 9. b 10. d

CD 內容

Track 007

（Peter：英國口音）

Janice: Can you speak Japanese?

Peter: Yes, I can, but not very well. Can you?

Janice: No, I can't. I can speak French, I can speak German, and I can also speak a little bit of Chinese, but I can't speak Japanese.

Peter: I see. Well, I can speak Japanese and Chinese fluently. I can't speak any European languages, except English of course. Can you read and write Chinese?

Janice: Mm. No, I can't. That's too difficult.

Peter: You can say that again!

Janice: And I can't be bothered. Can you read Chinese?

Peter: Yes, I can.

【中譯】

Janice: 你會說日語嗎？

Peter: 會，我會，可是說得沒有很好。妳會嗎？

Janice: 不，我不會。我會說法語，我會說德語，我也會說一點點中文，可是我不會說日語。

Peter: 這樣啊。呃，我的日語和中文都說得很流利。我不會說任何歐洲國家的語言，當然除了英文之外。妳可以閱讀和書寫中文嗎？

Janice: 嗯……不，我不行。太難了。

Peter: 你說的一點也沒錯！

Janice: 我才不自找麻煩呢。你可以閱讀中文嗎？

Peter: 行，我可以。

Track 008

US Affirmative 美式確定

/kæn/

I **can** hear you. 我可以聽見你。

US Negative 美式否定

/kænt/

I **can't** hear you. 我聽不見你。

US Question 美式問句

/kæn/

Can you hear me? 你聽得見我嗎？

US Alone 美式單獨使用

/kæn/

Yes, I **can**. 行，我可以。

UK Affirmative 英式確定

/kæn/

I **can** hear you. 我可以聽見你。

UK Negative 英式否定

/kɑnt/

I **can't** hear you. 我聽不見你。

UK Question 英式問句

/kæn/

Can you hear me? 你聽得見我嗎？

UK Alone 英式單獨使用

/kæn/

Yes, I **can**. 行，我可以。

Track 009

1. I can't run very fast.
2. I can cook spaghetti.
3. I can play the piano.
4. I can't eat raw fish.
5. I can sing the blues.
6. I can come tomorrow.
7. I can't tell you.
8. I can't swim very well.
9. I can't play cricket.
10. I can swim a hundred meters.
11. I can't read Chinese.
12. I can do that for you.

【中譯】

1. 我不能跑得很快。
2. 我會煮義大利麵。
3. 我會彈鋼琴。
4. 我不能吃生魚片。
5. 我會唱藍調歌曲。
6. 我明天可以來。
7. 我不能告訴你。
8. 我游得沒有很好。

9. 我不會打板球。

10. 我可以游一百公尺。

11. 我不會讀中文。

12. 那我可以幫你。

Track 010

1. I can't dive.
2. I can eat chocolate all the time.
3. I can type three hundred words a minute.
4. I can't speak German.
5. I can play the flute.
6. I can't make it then.
7. I can cook pizza.
8. I can't eat spicy food.
9. I can stand on my head.
10. I can't tell you.
11. I can't see very well without my glasses.
12. I can drive a truck.

【中譯】

1. 我不會潛水。
2. 我可以隨時都在吃巧克力。
3. 我一分鐘可以打 300 個字。
4. 我不會說德語。
5. 我會吹長笛。
6. 那我就辦不到了。
7. 我會做披薩。

8. 我不能吃辛辣的食物。
9. 我可以倒立。
10. 我不能告訴你。
11. 我沒戴眼鏡不能看得很清楚。
12. 我會開卡車。

Track 011

1. You can talk!
2. If you can't beat 'em, join 'em.
3. Can't win 'em all.
4. You can say that again!
5. I can't believe my ears!
6. Do it as best you can.
7. Can't hear myself think.
8. Nice work if you can get it.
9. You can bet your bottom dollar.
10. Can't be bothered.

【中譯】

1. 你會說話！（你真嘮叨！）
2. 打不過他們，就加入他們。（不能與之為敵，便與之為伍。）
3. 不可能全贏的。（人不可能事事都順心。）
4. 你可以再說一遍。（你說的一點都沒錯。）
5. 我不能相信我的耳朵。（我真不敢相信。）
6. 盡你最大的努力。
7. 聽不到我自己在想什麼。（這噪音吵得我心煩意亂。）
8. 如果你能得到，那就是好本事。（有本事就把它搞定。）

9. 你可以把口袋裡最後一塊錢拿來打賭。（我敢打包票。／我百分之百確定。）

10. 不能被這類事煩擾。（不想自找麻煩。）

Track 012

（Bob：英國口音）

Bob: Can you speak French?

Julie: Yes, I can.

Bob: Oh, cool. Can you translate this for me then?

Julie: Um, hang on, I can't see. Let me get my glasses. Where are they? I can't find them.

Bob: They're on your head.

Julie: Oh.

Bob: Gee, you always lose things like that!

Julie: Hey, you can talk! OK, let me take a look.

Bob: Can you see?

Julie: Yes. Um. I can't understand this.

Bob: But you told me you could translate it!

Julie: Well, yes I can, but I need my dictionary, otherwise I can't understand everything.

Bob: Here you are. Do the best you can.

【中譯】

Bob: 妳會說法語嗎？

Julie: 會，我會。

Bob: 哦，酷。那妳可以幫我翻譯這個嗎？

Julie: 嗯……等一下，我看不到。我拿一下我的眼鏡。眼鏡在哪裡？我找不到。

Bob: 在妳頭上。

Julie: 哦。

Bob: 哎呀，妳老是像這樣丟三落四的！

Julie: 嘿，你真嘮叨。好啦，讓我看看。

Bob: 妳看得見了嗎？

Julie: 對。呃……這我看不懂。

Bob: 可是妳跟我說妳可以翻譯的！

Julie: 呃，我是可以，可是我需要我的字典，要不然我不是什麼都看得懂。

Bob: 拿去。盡妳最大的努力吧。

Unit 4

Tea Or Coffee?

茶、還是咖啡？

學習重點 神奇的重音和語調

1 Mary 正在拜訪 Mark。請聽他們的對話，你可以聽懂多少呢？接著再聽第二遍，並試著完成下列表格，圈選出 Mary 在度假時所做的事情。 Track 013

聽聽看

	A	B
Is she drinking tea or coffee?	tea	coffee
Is she having milk tea or lemon tea?	milk	lemon
Did she go alone or with someone else?	alone	with someone else
Did she fly economy class or business class?	economy class	business class
Did it rain or was it sunny?	rain	sunny
Did she stay in a hotel or a hostel?	hotel	hostel
Did she rent a car or rent a bicycle?	rent a car	rent a bicycle
Did she drink light or dark beer?	light beer	dark beer

答案 請見65頁。

「or」在提供選項的問句中（如上列問句），有時候很難被聽到。如果你沒能聽見 or 這個字，你也許就會用 yes 或 no 來回答。這非常容易令人混淆！請再次聽 Mark 和 Mary 一開始的對話，你就會了解我的意思。這種混淆是相當常見的，因爲 or 常隱身在口說的句子中。讓我們先來看看它是怎麼發音的。

爲了清楚聽出 or，必須注意兩樣東西：語調和重音。讓我們先來看看語調的部分。

Or 通常位在兩個選項之間。第一個選項用上揚的語調說出，第二個選項則用下降的語調，如下：

Would you prefer coffee or tea?

藉由語調，可以清楚聽出問句中的選項： coffee 或 tea 。

至於重音， or 本身不是重讀的字，但它兩邊的選項都會重讀。 or 本身的發音非常快，聽起來就像：/ə/，如下：

Would you prefer COFFEE /ə/ TEA?

所以，要聽清楚此類提供選擇的問句，必須注意語調和重音，而不是 or 本身的發音。

聽聽看 2 聽的時候，請注意語調和重音。 Track 014

接著我們用一些簡單的問句來練習語調和重音。

說說看 3 請跟著 CD，一起覆誦下列簡單問句。 Track 015

1. Tea or coffee?
2. Milk or lemon?
3. Up or down?
4. Left or right?
5. Lost or stolen?
6. Me or you?
7. Him or her?
8. Us or them?
9. In or out?
10. My place or yours?

現在我們來挑戰更難的問句。記得，要留意語調和重音。

聽聽看

4 請聽 CD 播放的問句，並在下方表格圈選你所偏愛的選項。請看範例。 Track 016

	A	B
1	cats	dogs
2	iced coffee	hot coffee
3	pay by cash	pay by credit card
4	receipt	no receipt
5	sit inside	sit outside
6	play tennis	watch tennis
7	active vacations	relaxing vacations
8	swimming in the ocean	swimming in the pool
9	drink wine	drink beer
10	watch the movie first	read the book first

說說看

5 測試完聽力，這次請跟著 CD 覆誦這些問句。請盡量模仿 CD 的重音和語調。 Track 016

1. Do you prefer cats or are you more of a dog person?
2. Would you prefer iced coffee or hot coffee?
3. Are you paying by cash or credit card?
4. Do you need a receipt or not?
5. Would you like to sit inside or outside?
6. Do you prefer playing tennis, or just watching it on TV?

7. Do you like active vacations or relaxing vacations?
8. Do you prefer swimming in the ocean, or swimming in the pool?
9. Do you prefer to drink wine with your meal, or are you a beer drinker?
10. Do you prefer to watch the movie first and then read the book, or do you prefer to read the book first?

請先熟練前面所教的重點，因爲接下來的困難度愈來愈高了。能夠挑戰成功，恭喜，你的聽力又更上一層樓了。

聽聽看

6 請聽 CD 播放的問句，將問句的選項分別填在 A 、 B 欄，然後圈選你所偏愛的選項。 Track 017

	A	B
1		
2		
3		
4		
5		
6		
7		
8		
9		
10		

答案 請閱讀 71 頁的 CD 內容，看看你是否完全聽懂這些問句，然後用覆誦的方式練習說這些句子。

另外一個很難清楚聽見的小字是 of，但它卻非常重要。Of 永遠都是一個連結字，而且就像所有的連結字一樣，它的發音非常快。Of 在說話中有四個現象，使得它很難被清楚聽見。

1. 前行字的最後一個子音會和 of 連結，如：lots of 會變成 /lɑtsəv/。
2. 母音的發音是 /ə/。
3. /v/ 經常都不發音，所以 of 會變成只有 /ə/ 的音。
4. Of 前後的兩個字都會重讀。

讓我們來聽一些範例，你會更了解上述的現象。

聽聽看

7 聽第一遍時，請注意你聽到下列哪些字串。聽第二遍時，請試著將 of 後面所銜接的字寫出來。 Track 018

1. a great deal of ________
2. all kinds of ________
3. both of ________
4. lots of ________
5. most of ________
6. one of ________
7. plenty of ________
8. sorts of ________

答案 你可以閱讀 72 頁的 CD 內容，並核對答案。

聽聽看

8 請聽 CD 的唸法，並留意這些字串的連音方式。 Track 018

1. a great deal of rain
2. all kinds of beers
3. both of us
4. lots of milk

5. most of them

6. one of them

7. plenty of lovely cafes

8. sorts of cheeses

分析

聽的時候請注意下列重點：

1. Of 如何和前面的字連結。
2. Of 的母音變成了 /ə/；f 變成 /v/ 的音、有時候甚至快到聽不見。
3. Of 的前後兩個字都要重讀。
4. 聽完之後，請跟著覆誦幾次，記得，聽力和口說是正相關的二項能力喔。

Of 最常使用的時機之一，就是當我們在談論食物的時候。從下列的常用字串就可見一般。

動動腦 **9** 左側是一些常用的計量字串，請將它們與可搭配使用的食物名稱配對，可複選。如範例。

d i	1. a glass of	a) bread
____	2. a bag of	b) chips
____	3. a bottle of	c) chocolate
____	4. a piece of	d) milk
____	5. a bowl of	e) pickles
____	6. a loaf of	f) soup
____	7. a jar of	g) tea
____	8. a cup of	h) toast
____	9. a slice of	i) water

答案 請見 65 頁。核對完答案，請跟著 CD 覆誦這些字串。 **Track 019**

聽聽看

10 現在請聽另一段對話。聽的時候，請專注於本章的學習重點，看看你進步了多少。 **Track 020**

解答

聽聽看 1

	A	B
Is she drinking tea or coffee?	tea	coffee
Is she having milk tea or lemon tea?	milk	lemon
Did she go alone or with someone else?	alone	with someone else
Did she fly economy class or business class?	economy class	business class
Did it rain or was it sunny?	rain	sunny
Did she stay in a hotel or a hostel?	hotel	hostel
Did she rent a car or rent a bicycle?	rent a car	rent a bicycle
Did she drink light or dark beer?	light beer	dark beer

動動腦 9

1. **d、i** 2. **b** 3. **d、i** 4. **a、c** 5. **f**
6. **a** 7. **e** 8. **g** 9. **a、h**

CD 内容

Track 013

Mark: So how was your trip?

Mary: Oh, it was fabulous! You know, Europe!

Mark: Would you prefer coffee or tea?

Mary: Yes, please.

Mark: Huh? No, I mean coffee or tea.

Mary: Yes, that's fine. Oh, I see! I didn't hear you. Tea, please.

Mark: Milk or lemon?

Mary: Milk please, lots of milk.

Mark: A piece of cake?

Mary: Oh, lovely. Thanks.

Mark: Which airline did you fly?

Mary: We flew KLM to Amsterdam …

Mark: We? Did you go alone or with someone else?

Mary: I went with John.

Mark: Oh. Nice. Here.

Mary: Thanks.

Mark: Did you fly economy or business?

Mary: Economy. We aren't so rich.

Mark: Where did you go first?

Mary: Amsterdam! It was great, you know, plenty of lovely cafes, tons of bicycles, great shopping.

Mark: Did it rain or was it sunny?

Mary: It was sunny, which is surprising for Amsterdam, as there is usually a great deal of rain there. Can I have another piece of cake? It's delicious.

Mark: Of course, here you go. Another cup of tea?

Mary: Yes, thanks.

Mark: So, did you stay in a hotel, or in a hostel?

Mary: We stayed in three different hotels that John found on the internet. One of them was in a traditional Dutch house, with small, cosy rooms and high ceilings. You know, most of them are built next to a canal. They're so lovely. The houses are quite old, but all of them are so well looked after.

Mark: Did you rent a car or rent a bicycle?

Mary: We rented bicycles. Both of us had sore legs after the first day because we did so much cycling. We're not really used to that.

Mark: What was the food like?

Mary: Oh, great! Great beer!

Mark: Dark or light?

Mary: We drank mostly light beers, 'cause they're not so strong, but you can get all kinds of beers! And also, many different sorts of cheeses. You know Dutch cheese is really different from French cheese. It's lighter and not so stinky. We had lots!

【中譯】

Mark: 妳這趟旅遊好玩嗎？

Mary: 哦，棒透了！你知道的，歐洲欸！

Mark: 妳要喝咖啡或茶？

Mary: 好，麻煩你。

Mark: 啊？不，我是問咖啡或茶。

Mary: 對，好啊。哦，我知道了！我沒聽清楚。茶，麻煩你。

Mark: 加牛奶或檸檬？

Mary: 牛奶，多一點，麻煩你。

Mark: 要來塊蛋糕嗎？

Mary: 哦，太好了。謝謝。

Mark: 妳搭哪一家航空？

Mary: 我們搭荷蘭航空到阿姆斯特丹……

Mark: 我們？妳是一個人或是跟別人一起去的？

Mary: 我跟約翰一起去。

Mark: 哦，不錯嘛。給妳。

Mary: 謝謝。

Mark: 你們是坐經濟艙或商務艙？

Mary: 經濟艙。我們沒那麼有錢。

Mark: 你們第一個地方是去哪裡？

Mary: 阿姆斯特丹！很棒，你知道的，很多可愛的咖啡廳、超多的腳踏車、到處購物啊。

Mark: 那裡是雨天還是晴天？

Mary: 晴天，在阿姆斯特丹這很讓人意外呢，因為那裡常常下雨。可以再給我一塊蛋糕嗎？很好吃。

Mark: 當然，來，給妳。再來一杯茶？

Mary: 好，謝謝。

Mark: 那，你們是住飯店，還是青年旅館？

Mary: 我們住在三間不同的飯店，約翰在網路上找到的。一間是傳統的荷蘭房子，房間小小的、很舒適，天花板很高。你知道，那些房子大多蓋在運河旁邊，真的好棒喔。房子非常古老，不過都維護得很好。

Mark: 你們有租車或腳踏車嗎？

Mary: 我們租了腳踏車。我們兩個人第一天結束之後腿都痠了，因為我們騎了很久，不是很習慣那樣子騎。

Mark: 食物如何呢？

Mary: 哦，很棒！啤酒很好喝！

Mark: 黑啤酒還是淡啤酒？

Mary: 我們大多是喝淡啤酒，因為沒那麼烈，不過你在那裡可以買到各種啤酒！還有，各種不同的乳酪。荷蘭乳酪和法國乳酪真的很不一樣，口味比較淡，也比較沒那麼嗆鼻。我們吃了很多！

Track 014

Would your prefer coffee or tea?

你要喝咖啡或茶？

Track 015

1. Tea or coffee?
2. Milk or lemon?
3. Up or down?
4. Left or right?
5. Lost or stolen?
6. Me or you?
7. Him or her?
8. Us or them?
9. In or out?
10. My place or yours?

【中譯】

1. 茶或咖啡？
2. 牛奶或檸檬？
3. 上或下？

4. 左或右？
5. 掉了或被偷了？
6. 我或你？
7. 他或她？
8. 我們或他們？
9. 進或出？
10. 我家或你家？

Track 016

1. Do you prefer cats or are you more of a dog person?
2. Would you prefer iced coffee or hot coffee?
3. Are you paying by cash or credit card?
4. Do you need a receipt or not?
5. Would you like to sit inside or outside?
6. Do you prefer playing tennis, or just watching it on TV?
7. Do you like active holidays or relaxing holidays?
8. Do you prefer swimming in the ocean, or swimming in a pool?
9. Do you prefer to drink wine with your meal, or are you a beer drinker?
10. Do you prefer to watch the movie first and then read the book, or do you prefer to read the book first?

【中譯】

1. 你比較喜歡貓或者你是愛狗人士？
2. 你想要冰咖啡或熱咖啡？
3. 你要付現或刷卡？
4. 你需要收據還是不用？

5. 你要坐在裡面或外面？
6. 你喜歡打網球，還是看電視轉播？
7. 你喜歡動態的假期或是休息放鬆的假期？
8. 你喜歡在海裡游泳，還是在游泳池裡游泳？
9. 你喜歡用餐時喝葡萄酒，或者你是個愛喝啤酒的人？
10. 你喜歡先看電影再看書，還是你喜歡先看書？

Track 017

1. Do you prefer classical music or do you like listening to pop?
2. Do you think it's better to have children early, or do you think it's better to have them later in life?
3. Would you prefer to live in Europe, or do you think it would be better to live in America?
4. Do you think it's better for students to live in a dorm, or to live with their parents?
5. Would you prefer chicken or pork, madam?
6. Shall we have red wine, or would you rather have white?
7. Shall we go away for the weekend, or would you rather stay home and relax?
8. We could go and see a movie, or go to a bar. Which would you prefer?
9. Do you drive a scooter or a car?
10. Eat here or take away?

【中譯】

1. 你比較喜歡古典樂，或者你喜歡聽流行樂？
2. 你覺得早點生孩子比較好，還是你覺得晚一點生比較好？

3. 你喜歡住在歐洲，還是你覺得住在美國比較好？
4. 你認為學生住在宿舍比較好，或是跟父母住？
5. 你想要雞肉或豬肉，女士？
6. 我們來喝紅酒吧，還是你比較喜歡白酒？
7. 我們週末出去玩吧，還是你比較想在家放鬆休息？
8. 我們可以去看場電影，或是去酒吧。你比較喜歡哪一個？
9. 你是騎機車或開車？
10. 內用還是外帶？

Track 018

1. a great deal of rain
2. all kinds of beers
3. both of us
4. lots of milk
5. most of them
6. one of them
7. plenty of lovely cafes
8. sorts of cheeses

【中譯】

1. 大量的雨
2. 各種啤酒
3. 我們兩個人（都）
4. 很多牛奶
5. 他們大多數人
6. 他們之一
7. 許多可愛的咖啡店
8. 各種乳酪

Track 019

1. a glass of water
2. a glass of milk
3. a bag of chips
4. a bottle of milk
5. a bottle of water
6. a piece of chocolate
7. a piece of bread
8. a bowl of soup
9. a loaf of bread
10. a jar of pickles

11. a cup of tea

12. a slice of toast

13. a slice of bread

【中譯】

1. 一杯水
2. 一杯牛奶
3. 一包薯片
4. 一瓶牛奶
5. 一瓶水
6. 一塊巧克力
7. 一塊麵包
8. 一碗湯
9. 一條麵包
10. 一罐醃菜
11. 一杯茶
12. 一片土司
13. 一片麵包

Track 020

Mark: So where did you go after Amsterdam?

Mary: Oh, we went to Paris. You know the great thing about Europe is that you can get to all of these places very quickly.

Mark: So how did you get there? Did you fly or take the train?

Mary: We took the train.

Mark: First class, or second class?

Mary: Oh, third class. Can I have a slice of that toast? I'm rather hungry.

Mark: Of course, here you go.

Mary: Thanks.

Mark: So do they use Francs in France now, or is it all the Euro?

Mary: Oh no, it's the Euro wherever you go, so it's very convenient. You don't have to keep changing money.

Mark: Oh that's good. Was Paris more expensive, or was Amsterdam, would you say?

Mary: Oh, I think Paris was more expensive. We had a more expensive hotel, so most of our budget was spent on the hotel.

Mark: Oh, I see. Was it a four star hotel or a five star hotel?

Mary: Five star.

Mark: Oh my god! That must have been really pricey. Was it downtown or in the suburbs?

Mary: Downtown. Near the Eiffel Tower.

Mark: Nice. So what did you do in Paris? Museums or shopping?

Mary: Both. The galleries are fabulous there. We also went to quite a few of the wine producers who have shops in Paris. We bought so many bottles of wine! You know, John likes his wine.

Mark: Did you buy white wine or red wine?

Mary: Well, John thinks French red wines are better than white, so he bought tons of red.

Mark: Did he buy bottles or those boxes they have in Europe, you know? Those boxes of wine?

Mary: Oh bottles. Our luggage was really heavy on the way back!

Mark: I can imagine!

【中譯】

Mark: 阿姆斯特丹之後，你們去了哪裡？

Mary: 哦，我們去了巴黎。關於歐洲最棒的事情，就是你可以很快地到達所有地方。

Mark: 那你們是怎麼到那裡的？你們是搭飛機或搭火車？

Mary: 我們搭火車。

Mark: 頭等車廂或二等車廂？

Mary: 哦，三等車廂。我可以來一片土司嗎？我挺餓的。

Mark: 當然，來，給妳。

Mary: 謝謝。

Mark: 那現在法國是用法朗，還是全部都用歐元？

Mary: 哦，沒有，你到哪裡都是用歐元，所以很方便。你不必一直兌換貨幣。

Mark: 哦，那不錯。妳說是巴黎比較貴，還是阿姆斯特丹呢？

Mary: 哦，我覺得巴黎比較貴。我們住的是比較貴的飯店，所以大部分的預算都是花在飯店住宿。

Mark: 哦，這樣啊。那是四星級飯店還是五星級飯店？

Mary: 五星級。

Mark: 哦，我的天啊！那真的要花很多錢。是在市區或是在郊區？

Mary: 市區。靠近艾菲爾鐵塔。

Mark: 不賴哩。那你們在巴黎做了些什麼？參觀博物館還是購物？

Mary: 都有。那裡的美術館棒透了。我們也去了不少在巴黎開店的葡萄酒製造廠。我們買了很多瓶葡萄酒。你知道的，約翰很喜歡葡萄酒。

Mark: 你們買的是白酒還是紅酒？

Mary: 呃，約翰認為法國的紅酒比白酒好，所以他買了很多紅酒。

Mark: 他買的是瓶裝的，還是你知道的，歐洲那種盒裝的？那些木盒葡萄酒？

Mary: 哦，瓶裝的。我們回程的行李箱可是很重哩！

Mark: 我可以想像！

Unit 5

He's a Great Actor, Isn't He?
他是很棒的演員，不是嗎？

學習重點 附加問句的弦外之音

聽聽看

1 Susan 和 George 正在談論蝙蝠俠電影。請聽他們的對話，你能聽懂多少呢？接著再聽一遍，這一次請判斷下列句子的陳述是 True 還是 False 。 Track 021

____ **1.** Susan thinks Heath Ledger is the best villain in all the Batman movies.

____ **2.** George thinks Jack Nicholson is not as good as Heath Ledger.

____ **3.** There are three Batman movies.

____ **4.** All the Batman movies are directed by the same director.

____ **5.** Christopher Nolan directed the last two Batman movies.

____ **6.** *The Dark Knight* was the first time Christian Bale played Batman.

____ **7.** George is passionate about movies.

答案 請閱讀 86 頁的 CD 內容檢查你的答案。

注意到了嗎，George 和 Susan 之間的對話進行得很順暢，因爲他們兩個人都使用了附加問句，鼓勵對方作出回應。附加問句是幫助對話流暢進行、並讓說話者在對話中感覺自在的好方法。

聽聽看

2 請再聽一次對話，這一次專注在附加問句上，將你所聽到的附加問句打勾。 Track 021

Don't you?		Wasn't she?	
Do you?		Hasn't he?	

Isn't it?		Doesn't it?	
Aren't they?		Wasn't he?	
Aren't you?		Aren't there?	
Didn't you?		Haven't you?	
Isn't he?		Didn't they?	

答案 請見85頁。

附加問句的規則很容易搞混，因此除非你很有把握，不然建議你不要使用，免得自找麻煩。然而，**聽懂**附加問句卻很重要，因爲你必須以正確的方式做出回應。

不以文法的角度來看，附加問句可分爲兩種。**第一種是用來問問題的附加問句**，當說話者眞的不知道答案，而希望你提供訊息時使用。**第二種是用來確認答案**，當說話者假設他已經知道答案，但是希望你確認答案時使用。

用來問問題的附加問句，語調會上揚，就像這樣：

I think he's great, don't you? ↗

用來確認答案的附加問句，語調會下降，就像這樣：

You like cheese, don't you? ↘

能夠聽出其中的差異很重要，因爲聽懂了，你才能做出正確的回應。

3 請再聽一次對話，判斷下列句子的附加問句，語調是上揚還是下降呢。請看範例。 Track 021

上揚 **1.** Heath Ledger was the Joker, wasn't he?

______ **2.** He was really great, wasn't he?

______ **3.** He's really good at acting crazy, isn't he?

______ **4.** He's quite old now, isn't he?

______ **5.** There are three of them, aren't there?

______ **6.** There are seven, aren't there?

______ **7.** They all had different directors, didn't they?

______ **8.** They worked together before, didn't they?

______ **9.** You know a lot about movies, don't you?

______ **10.** You love Batman too, don't you?

答案 請見85頁。如果無法聽出所有的語調差別，請多練習幾次。

4 現在請練習將上一題的句子和附加問句用正確的語調說出來。記得，語調可以誇張一些，你的意思較能清楚傳達。 Track 022

現在我們來學習以正確的方式做出回應。如果是用來問問題的附加問句，你只須針對問句本身回答，不必理會附加問句，例如：Taiwan is not a member of the WHO, is it? No, it's not. 或 Taiwan is not a member of the WTO, is it? Yes, it is actually.。

說說看

5 請聽問句，並以適當的方式回答問題。請見下列範例。

Track 023

Q : Taiwan is an island, isn't it?

A : Yes, that's right!

小叮嚀

如果無法聽清楚問題，可以多練習幾次。如果仍有困難，再翻閱本章末的 CD 內容。

用來確認答案的附加問句比較困難，因爲有時候說話者的假設是正確的，有時候則是錯誤的。

如果說話者的假設是正確的，而附加問句是否定型，那麼你就必須肯定地回應。

例 1 **Q : You like her, don't you?** 你喜歡她，不是嗎？

A : Oh yes, very much! 是的，非常喜歡！

例 2 **Q : You've seen this before, haven't you?**

你以前看過這個，不是嗎？

A : Yes, a few times, actually. 是的，其實看過幾次了。

如果說話者的假設是正確的，而附加問句是肯定型，那麼你就必須否定地回應。

例 1 **Q : You didn't know that, did you?** 你不知道那個，對嗎？

A : No, I didn't. 不，我不知道。

例2 **Q：You don't like coffee, do you?** 你不喜歡咖啡，對嗎？

A：Not really, no. 不，不是很喜歡。

如果說話者的假設是錯誤的，你可以簡單的說：Well, actually yes. 或 Well, actually no.，然後以和附加問句相同的型式來回應，請看以下範例，你會有更清楚的概念。

例1 **Q：You've been to the U.S. before, haven't you?**

你以前去過美國，不是嗎？

A：Well, no actually, I haven't.

嗯，事實上沒有，我沒去過。

例2 **Q：You haven't read this yet, have you?**

你還沒讀過這個，對嗎？

A：Well, yes, actually, I have. 嗯，事實上有，我讀過了。

所以，結論就是：聽到用來確認答案的附加問句，如果假設是「正確」的，你的回答就必須跟附加問句「相反」；如果假設是「不正確」的，你的回答就必須跟附加問句「相同」。懂了嗎？

動動腦 6 上述說明整理成如下表格，請看看你是否都了解了。

用來確認答案的附加問句

	A 說話者	B 說話者
正確的假設		
否定的附加問句	You like her, don't you? She's great, isn't she?	→Oh yes, very much! →She's super!

肯定的附加問句	You didn't know that, did you? You aren't Japanese, are you?	→ No, I didn't. → No, I'm not.
不正確的假設		
否定的附加問句	You've been to the U.S. before, haven't you? You met him, didn't you?	→ Well, no actually, I haven't. → Well, no actually, I didn't.
肯定的附加問句	You haven't read this yet, have you? They weren't there, were they?	→ Well, yes, actually, I have. → Well, yes, actually, they were.

讓我們來練習回應此類附加問句。

說說看

7 請聽用來確認答案的附加問句，並練習做出回答。

Track 024

小叮嚀

如果無法完全聽懂問題，請多練習幾次。如果仍有困難，可參閱本章末的 CD 內容。

先前提過，如果你對於附加問句規則沒有完全的把握，就不要使用它。要取代附加問句，你可以使用以下的慣用語來幫助對話順利進行。這些慣用語和附加問句有相同的功能，不過它們比較簡單，不容易犯錯。

說說看

8 請跟著 CD 覆誦下列用語，請特別留意語調的使用。

Track 025

- **Don't you think?** 你不這麼認為嗎？
- **You know?** 你知道的？
- **Do you know what I mean?** 你知道我的意思嗎？
- **Right?** 對嗎？

聽聽看

9 現在請聽另一段對話。聽的時候，請專注於本章的學習重點，看看你進步了多少。 Track 026

解答

聽聽看 2

Don't you?	✔	Wasn't she?	
Do you?		Hasn't he?	
Isn't it?		Doesn't it?	
Aren't they?		Wasn't he?	✔
Aren't you?		Aren't there?	✔
Didn't you?		Haven't you?	
Isn't he?	✔	Didn't they?	✔

聽聽看 3

1. 上揚
2. 下降
3. 下降
4. 上揚
5. 上揚
6. 下降
7. 上揚
8. 下降
9. 下降
10. 上揚

CD 內容

Track 025

（George ：英國口音）

說明 用來問問題的附加問句以底線標示；用來確認答案的附加問句以套色標示。

Susan: Have you seen the new Batman movie?

George: Yes. I loved it! What did you think of it?

Susan: Well, it was OK, but I thought it was too long, you know?

George: No, I thought it was too short! Heath Ledger was the Joker, wasn't he?

Susan: Yes, he was really great, wasn't he?

George: Yes, brilliant.

Susan: I thought he was the best villain in all the Batman movies, don't you think?

George: Well, actually, I think Jack Nicholson was good as the first Joker. You know, he was quite crazy in that part. He's really good at acting crazy, isn't he?

Susan: Oh yes, he is. He's quite old now, isn't he?

George: Mmm, about 70, I think. So what's your favorite Batman movie?

Susan: Oh mm, let me see. There are three of them, aren't there?

George: Actually, there are seven, aren't there?

Susan: Seven! You're kidding me!

George: Well, yes, some early ones which no one has ever seen, you know, black and white movies.

Susan: They all had different directors, didn't they?

George: Well, yes, Christopher Nolan directed the last two, *Batman Begins* and *The Dark Knight*.

Susan: Oh, OK, and he and the actor, what's his name, Christian Bale, they worked together before, didn't they?

George: Yes, they made *Batman Begins* together.

Susan: Wow, you know a lot about movies, don't you?

George: Well, it's kind of my passion, do you know what I mean? But, look, everyone loves movies, right? I mean, you love Batman too, don't you?

Susan: Oh, of course!

【中譯】

Susan: 你看過新的那部《蝙蝠俠》電影嗎？

George: 有。我超愛的！妳覺得怎樣？

Susan: 呃，還可以，不過我認為片子太長了，對吧？

George: 才不，我認為太短了！希斯．萊傑就是「小丑」，對嗎？

Susan: 對啊，他真的很棒，對吧？

George: 對啊，棒透了。

Susan: 我認為他是《蝙蝠俠》電影裡面演得最好的壞蛋，你不認為嗎？

George: 呃，事實上，我覺得第一位演「小丑」的傑克．尼克遜演得很好。妳知道的，他的那個角色相當瘋狂。他真的很會演瘋狂的角色，對吧？

Susan: 就是啊，他真的很會演。他現在很老了，對嗎？

George: 嗯……大概七十了，我想。那妳最喜歡的《蝙蝠俠》電影是哪一部？

Susan: 噢，嗯……我想想。一共有三部，對吧？

George: 事實上，有七部，不是嗎？

Susan: 七部！你在開玩笑！

George: 是真的，早期的幾部電影沒有人看過，妳知道的，黑白電影。

Susan: 它們每一部的導演都不一樣，對嗎？

George: 對啊，克里斯多福．諾藍導演最後兩部，《開戰時刻》和《黑暗騎士》。

Susan: 哦，對，而且他和那個演員，他叫什麼名字來著，克利斯汀．貝爾，他們以前合作過，對吧？

George: 對，他們一起拍攝《開戰時刻》。

Susan: 哇，你知道很多電影的東西呢，對吧？

George: 噢，這有點算是我的愛好，妳知道我的意思吧？可是，嘿，每個人都愛電影，對吧？我是說，妳也愛蝙蝠俠，不是嗎？

Susan: 哦，當然！

Track 022

說明 用來問問題的附加問句以底線標示；用來確認答案的附加問句以套色標示。

1. Heath Ledger was the Joker, <u>wasn't he</u>?
2. He was really great, wasn't he?
3. He's really good at acting crazy, isn't he?
4. He's quite old now, <u>isn't he</u>?
5. There are three of them, <u>aren't there</u>?
6. There are seven, aren't there?
7. They all had different directors, <u>didn't they</u>?
8. They worked together before, didn't they?
9. You know a lot about movies, don't you?
10. You love Batman too, <u>don't you</u>?

【中譯】

1. 希斯・萊傑就是「小丑」，不是嗎？
2. 他真的很棒，對吧？
3. 他真的很會演瘋狂的角色，不是嗎？
4. 他現在很老了，不是嗎？
5. 一共有三部，不是嗎？
6. 有七部，不是嗎？
7. 它們每一部的導演都不一樣，不是嗎？
8. 他們以前合作過，不是嗎？
9. 你知道很多電影的東西，不是嗎？
10. 你也愛蝙蝠俠，不是嗎？

Track 023

1. Taiwan is an island, isn't it?
2. It's hot in August, isn't it?
3. Batman was played by Brad Pitt, wasn't he?
4. You went to school in the US, didn't you?
5. You have seen the new *Batman* movie, haven't you?
6. You have three sisters, don't you?
7. Your father is German, isn't he?
8. The last Olympics was in Beijing, wasn't it?
9. Tea is grown in Taiwan, isn't it?
10. Al Pacino is an actor, isn't he?

【中譯】

1. 台灣是一座島，不是嗎？
2. 八月的天氣很熱，不是嗎？

3. 蝙蝠俠是布萊德·彼特演的，不是嗎？
4. 你是在美國求學的，不是嗎？
5. 你看過新的那部《蝙蝠俠》電影了，不是嗎？
6. 你有三個姐妹，不是嗎？
7. 你父親是德國人，不是嗎？
8. 最後一次奧運是在北京，不是嗎？
9. 茶是在台灣栽種的，不是嗎？
10. 艾爾·帕西諾是一位演員，不是嗎？

Track 024

1. You are Taiwanese, aren't you?
2. You're not Japanese, are you?
3. You speak Mandarin, don't you?
4. You're studying English, aren't you?
5. You've studied it before, haven't you?
6. You are going to the US to do your master's, aren't you?
7. Brad Pitt is a politician, isn't he?
8. Germany is in South America, isn't it?
9. Taiwan is a very cold country, isn't it?
10. You went to a disco last night, didn't you?

【中譯】

1. 你是台灣人，不是嗎？
2. 你不是日本人，對吧？
3. 你會說國語，不是嗎？
4. 你正在學英文，不是嗎？
5. 你以前學過了，不是嗎？

6. 你打算去美國讀碩士，不是嗎？
7. 布萊德・彼特是個政治人物，不是嗎？
8. 德國是在南美洲，不是嗎？
9. 台灣是一個天氣很冷的國家，不是嗎？
10. 你昨晚去迪斯可舞廳，不是嗎？

Track 026

（George ：英國口音）

說明 用來問問題的附加問句以底線標示；用來確認答案的附加問句以套色標示。

Susan: So, in your opinion, George, as a film buff, what's the greatest movie of all time?

George: Well, what do you think?

Susan: Oh, it's probably *The Godfather*, isn't it?

George: Well, yes, in my view it is. What about you? You've seen it, haven't you?

Susan: Oh yes, of course.

George: It's magnificent, isn't it?

Susan: Yes, I have to say it is. I've seen it so many times and each time I see it, I'm impressed by how good it is.

George: What makes it so good?

Susan: I think it's the attention to detail, you know?

George: Oh, interesting.

Susan: Also, it was the first movie for many of those involved, wasn't it?

George: Yes, the director's first movie, Al Pacino's first movie, Diane

Keaton's first movie. But the book was already very famous, wasn't it?

Susan: Yes, it was. It was a surprise bestseller. You've read it, haven't you?

George: Actually, well, no, I haven't.

Susan: Oh, it's a good read, of course not as good as the movie, do you know what I mean?

George: So which of the three parts of *The Godfather* do you think is the best?

Susan: Well, I actually think Part II is the best, don't you?

George: Mm. Why?

Susan: The way the two stories work together is so well done, don't you think?

George: Right! Robert De Niro and Al Pacino were so good together, weren't they?

Susan: You see that's interesting because you know they never appear in the same scene together in that movie, don't you?

George: But they were in that movie together, weren't they?

Susan: They were in the same movie, but they never acted together in it.

George: Oh interesting, I never realized that!

【中譯】

Susan: 那，George，身為一位電影愛好者，史上最偉大的電影是哪一部呢？

George: 呃，妳認為呢？

Susan: 哦，應該是《教父》，對吧？

George: 呃，是啊，依我看就是這部。妳認為呢？妳看過這部電影，對嗎？

Susan: 對啊，當然。

George: 是一部鉅作，對嗎？

Susan: 是，我必須說的確是。我看過很多次，每一次我都會讚嘆它拍的真好。

George: 它這麼好的原因是什麼？

Susan: 我認為是因為細節都處理得很好，你了解吧？

George: 嗯，有意思。

Susan: 而且，裡頭很多人都是第一次拍電影，不是嗎？

George: 是啊，那是導演的第一部電影、艾爾．帕西諾的第一部電影、黛安．基頓的第一部電影。不過它的書已經很有名了，對嗎？

Susan: 是，沒錯。那是一本讓人意外的暢銷書。你讀過了，對吧？

George: 事實上，呃，沒有，我還沒讀過。

Susan: 噢，那是一本好書，當然，還是沒有電影好看，你知道我的意思吧？

George: 那三集《教父》的電影，妳認為哪一集最好看？

Susan: 呃，事實上我認為第二集最好看，你不認為嗎？

George: 嗯……為什麼？

Susan: 兩個故事串連得很好，你不覺得嗎？

George: 就是啊！勞勃．狄尼洛和艾爾．帕西諾合作無間，對吧？

Susan: 你看，那很有意思喔，因為你知道的，他們在那部電影從來沒有同時出現在同一個場景，對吧？

George: 不過他們都有演那部電影，不是嗎？

Susan: 他們都有演這一部電影，不過他們在戲裡都沒有對手戲。

George: 哦，有意思，我從來沒有注意過呢！

Part 2

會議篇

Meeting

Unit 6

When Is the Meeting Starting?

會議什麼時候開始？

學習重點 問句語調往上或往下，有差別！

聽聽看

1 **Julie 和 Brian 正在開會。請聽會議的對談，你可以聽懂多少？接著再聽一遍，這次請留意他們彼此提出的問題。**

Track 027

答案 請閱讀 107 頁的 CD 內容。

在 Unit 2，我們學過以問句中的助動詞來幫助你了解問題。在這個單元，我們要延伸學習，在聽問題時多留意另一件事，那就是「語調」。

問句有兩種基本的語調模式：

❶ 語調上揚的問句：

通常是 yes/no 問句，問話者期待的是一個 yes/no 的回答。請看範例：

例 1

Q：Are you going to the meeting tomorrow?

你明天會參加會議嗎？

A：No, unfortunately, I can't make it.

不會，很不巧，我不能參加。

例 2

Q：Do you have any messages for me?

你有任何要給我的留言嗎？

A：Um, yes, here you are.

嗯，有，在這裡。

❷ 語調下降的問句：

通常是 wh- 問句，問話者期待的是問句中所要求的資訊。請見範例：

例 1

Q：When are you arriving?

你何時會到達？

A：I think my flight gets in at 6:30.

我想我的班機 6:30 會到。

例 2

Q：Who else is going to be there?

其他還有誰會去？

A：John and Tracy will both be there.

John 和 Tracy 都會去。

了解這一點很有用，因為即使你無法聽懂問題中的每一個字，還是可以藉由語調模式，幫助你了解問題並思考適當的回答方式。

動動腦 **2** 請看下列問句，它們分別是 yes/no 還是 wh- 問句呢，請在正確欄位打 ✔。

		yes/no	wh-
1	Is this the right one?	✔	
2	Where is Tracy today?		
3	What happened to the minutes from the last meeting?		

		yes/no	wh-
4	Are we all here?		
5	Did you receive the agenda?		
6	When did you get the figures?		
7	Who is taking notes today?		
8	Have you read the report?		
9	Are you meeting Judy this afternoon?		
10	What is the figure on page 7?		

答案 請見 106 頁。

聽聽看

3 現在請聽上列問句的語調，可以跟著覆誦幫助自己更熟悉這些語調。 Track 028

聽聽看

4 請聽 CD 播出的問句，它們分別是 yes/no 還是 wh- 問句呢，請在正確欄位打 ✔ 。接著再聽一遍，這次請試著將你聽到的問句寫出來，完成下列表格。 Track 029

		yes/no	wh-
1			
2			
3			
4			
5			
6			
7			

		yes/no	wh-
8			
9			
10			

答案 請見 106 頁。

說說看

5 能夠聽出這些問句後，接著練習用相同的語調說出這些句子，請跟著 CD 覆誦。 Track 029

有時候，問句其實是一項請求。使用此類問句，發問者並不期待任何資訊或是 yes/no 的回答，而是希望你同意做某件事。此類問句句尾的語調通常會上揚。

例 1

Q：Do you think you could help me with this?
你覺得你可以幫我做這件事嗎？

A：Sure. What can I do?
當然，我可以做些什麼？

例 2

Q：Can you be responsible for this?
你可以負責這件事嗎？

A：Sure. No problem.
當然，沒問題。

說說看

6 請研讀下列這些可以用來「表示請求」的字串。請跟著 CD 覆誦來練習發音。 Track 030

- Do you think you could …?
- Would it be possible for you to …?
- Could you …?
- Can you …?

聽聽看

7 請聽 CD 播放的問句，並以適當方式回答。 Track 031

答案 這些問題的類型都不相同，有的須針對問題提供資訊、有的以 yes 或 no 回答、或是以 Sure! 回答表示同意做某件事。如果你覺得這個練習很難，可以閱讀 112 頁的 CD 內容。

想要更熟練這些表示請求的用語，可以回頭再聽聽 Track 027，看看你可以聽出它們嗎？也可搭配本章末的 CD 內容，學習它們的用法。

有時候，你需要時間思考答案，或者你想要確認你了解問題後再回答，那麼有兩個技巧你可以使用：

1. 當你思考如何回答問題的時候，可以暫緩回應，例如：

Q： Who else is going to be there?
其他還有誰會去？

A： Mmm, let me see. John, and Tracy.
嗯……我想想，John 和 Tracy 會去。

2. 你可以請發問者把問題再說一遍，例如：

Q：When are you arriving?
你何時抵達？

A：Sorry, can you say that again?
不好意思，你可以再說一次嗎？

在你想要使用這二個技巧時，下列字串可以派上用場。

動動腦 **8 請閱讀下列字串，你能分辨它們屬於哪一種類別嗎，請將它們分類填入下方表格。**

- I'm afraid I don't quite follow.
- It depends what you mean by that.
- Mmm, let me see.
- Mmm, well, I'm not sure. I think ...
- Oh well, you know, um …
- Sorry, can you say that again?
- Sorry, you mean …?
- Sorry, what do you mean?
- Well, it's kind of hard to say.
- Pardon me?

延遲回答字串	重複問題字串

答案 請核對你的答案，並研讀下方的重點提醒。

延遲回答字串	重複問題字串
• **Mmm, let me see.** 嗯，讓我想想……	• **I'm afraid I don't quite follow.** 我恐怕沒聽清楚。
• **Mmm, well, I'm not sure. I think ...** 嗯，好，我不是很確定，我想……	• **Sorry, can you say that again?** 不好意思，你可以再說一遍嗎？
• **It depends what you mean by that.** 要看你所指為何。	• **Sorry, what do you mean?** 不好意思，你的意思是什麼？
• **Well, it's kind of hard to say.** 嗯，這很難說呢。	• **Sorry, you mean ...?** 不好意思，你指的是……？
• **Oh well, you know, um ...** 喔，好，你知道的，嗯……	• **Pardon me?** 不好意思，可以再說一遍嗎？

分析

- 注意，當你想拖延回答時，不可以說：Me?「我喔？」。舉例來說，Q：Are you going to the meeting tomorrow?「問：你明天要參加會議嗎？」A：Me? ...「答：我喔？……」。對說中文的人來說，這是很普遍的暫緩回答技巧，不過這樣的英文聽起來很奇怪。
- 注意，如果你想請對方重複一遍，不要只說 What?「什麼？」或是 Huh?「啊？」，這是不禮貌的。在平常的社交場合也許行得通，但在正式的商務會議上就不恰當了。

說說看

9 現在請跟著 CD，練習這些字串的說法。

Track 032

想要更熟悉這些字串的使用方式，可以回頭聽聽 Track 027，你可以聽出幾個字串呢？如果需要，可以對照本單元後面的 CD 內容。

聽聽看

10 請聽 CD 播放的問句，並以適當方式回答。

Track 033

答案 聽的時候請留意語調。先練習使用延遲回答或重複問題字串，接著再針對問題回答。這些問題的類型都不相同，有的須針對問題提供資訊、有的以 yes 或 no 回答、或是以 Sure! 回答表示同意做某件事。如果你覺得這個練習很難，可以閱讀 114 頁的 CD 內容。

聽聽看

11 請聽 Macey 、 Steve 和 Mike 之間的會議對談。請專注於本單元所學到的重點，看看你進步了多少。

Track 034

解答

動動腦 2

		yes/no	wh-
1	Is this the right one?	✔	
2	Where is Tracy today?		✔
3	What happened to the minutes from the last meeting?		✔
4	Are we all here?	✔	
5	Did you receive the agenda?	✔	
6	When did you get the figures?		✔
7	Who is taking notes today?		✔
8	Have you read the report?	✔	
9	Are you meeting Judy this afternoon?	✔	
10	What is the figure on page 7?		✔

聽聽看 4

		yes/no	wh-
1	What are the figures for last month?		✔
2	Are we having a break for coffee?	✔	
3	Did you get my last email?	✔	
4	When are we meeting the client?		✔
5	Where did the last meeting take place?		✔
6	Is the handout ready?	✔	
7	Has anyone checked the equipment?	✔	
8	Who is going to take responsibility for this?		✔
9	Are there any questions about the graph?	✔	
10	How long have we got?		✔

CD 內容

Track 027

Julie: So how are we doing with the arrangements for the conference next week?

Brian: Well, the invitations have been sent out.

Julie: Who have we had responses from?

Brian: Mmm, let me see … George from TSC, Mary from BDE, and June from TSO have all accepted.

Julie: Has anyone declined?

Brian: Yes, Tracy from TSM can't make it. She's on a business trip at that time.

Julie: OK. Has the meeting room been booked?

Brian: Yes. And the equipment has been checked.

Julie: Who is going to be our keynote speaker?

Brian: Sorry, what do you mean?

Julie: Who is going to be our keynote speaker?

Brian: I thought you were.

Julie: Me? Oh no, I thought we were going to invite someone to do that.

Brian: Really? Well, no one told me.

Julie: OK, so we need to book someone. Any ideas who?

Brian: We could ask our CEO?

Julie: Oh, that's a good idea.

Brian: Do you think you could ask him?

Julie: OK, I'll speak to him this afternoon. What about the caterers? Who are we using this time to provide the food and drink?

Brian: Same company as last time.

Julie: What kind of food did you order? Chinese or Western?

Brian: We had Chinese last time, so I ordered Western food this time.

Julie: Is it the same price?

Brian: Mmm, well, I'm not sure. I think it's more or less the same.

Julie: Can you check?

Brian: Sure.

Julie: Are there any vegetarians?

Brian: I'm afraid I don't quite follow.

Julie: We need to check if any of our guests are vegetarian, and make sure there is enough vegetarian food for them.

Brian: Oh yes, good point.

【中譯】

Julie: 關於下週的會議，我們安排得如何了？

Brian: 呃，邀請函已經寄出了。

Julie: 我們有收到誰的回覆嗎？

Brian: 嗯，我看看…… TSC 的 George、BDE 的 Mary 和 TSO 的 June，都接受邀請了。

Julie: 有誰回絕嗎？

Brian: 有，TSM 的 Tracy 沒辦法出席。她那個時間在出差。

Julie: 好。會議室已經預約了嗎？

Brian: 是。而且設備都已經確認過了。

Julie: 誰會是我們的主講人？

Brian: 對不起，妳的意思是什麼？

Julie: 誰是我們的主講人。

Brian: 我以為是妳啊。

Julie: 我？哦不，我以為我們要邀請別人來主講啊。

Brian: 真的嗎？呃，沒人跟我說。

Julie: 好，所以我們必須預約某個人。有想到誰嗎？

Brian: 我們可以邀請我們的執行長？

Julie: 哦，這是個好意見。

Brian: 妳想妳可以問問他嗎？

Julie: 好，我今天下午跟他談。外燴公司呢？我們這次要請誰提供餐點和飲料？

Brian: 跟上次同一家公司。

Julie: 你訂了哪一種餐點？中式或西式？

Brian: 我們上一次是中式的，所以我這次訂了西式餐點。

Julie: 價錢一樣嗎？

Brian: 嗯，呃……我不確定。我想或多或少是一樣的吧。

Julie: 你可以查一下嗎？

Brian: 沒問題。

Julie: 有任何人吃素嗎？

Brian: 我恐怕不是很確定妳的意思。

Julie: 我們必須確認我們的來賓是不是有誰吃素，要確定幫他們準備足夠的素食餐點。

Brian: 哦對，有道理。

Track 028

1. Is this the right one?
2. Where is Tracy today?
3. What happened to the minutes from the last meeting?
4. Are we all here?
5. Did you receive the agenda?
6. When did you get the figures?

7. Who is taking notes today?

8. Have you read the report?

9. Are you meeting Judy this afternoon?

10. What is the figure on page 7?

【中譯】

1. 是這個嗎？
2. Tracy 今天在哪？
3. 上次開會的記錄怎麼了？
4. 我們大伙都到了嗎？
5. 你們有拿到會議議程嗎？
6. 你什麼時候拿到這個數據？
7. 今天誰做記錄？
8. 你看過報告了嗎？
9. 你今天下午要和 Judy 會面嗎？
10. 第七頁是什麼數字？

Track 029

1. What are the figures for last month?

2. Are we having a break for coffee?

3. Did you get my last email?

4. When are we meeting the client?

5. Where did the last meeting take place?

6. Is the handout ready?

7. Has anyone checked the equipment?

8. Who is going to take responsibility for this?

9. Are there any questions about the graph?

10. How long have we got?

【中譯】

1. 上個月的數字是多少？
2. 我們要休息喝個咖啡嗎？
3. 你有沒有收到我的上一封電子郵件？
4. 我們什麼時候要和客戶會面？
5. 上一場會議是在哪裡舉行的？
6. 講義準備好了嗎？
7. 有人檢查過設備了嗎？
8. 誰要負責這件事？
9. 關於這張圖表有任何問題嗎？
10. 我們有多少時間？

Track 031

1. Have you traveled abroad on business this year?

2. When did you start your current job?

3. Do you get along with your colleagues?

4. Who do you work for?

5. Did you have a meeting today?

6. How often do you attend meetings in English?

7. Do you think you could recommend this book to your friend?

8. Are you happy in your job?

9. Would it be possible for you to help me?

10. What time do you start work in the morning?

【中譯】

1. 你今年到海外出差過了嗎？
2. 你目前的工作是從什麼時候開始的？
3. 你跟同事們相處的好嗎？
4. 你為誰工作？
5. 你今天要開會嗎？
6. 你多久參加一次英文會議？
7. 你想你可以推薦這本書給你的朋友嗎？
8. 你工作愉快嗎？
9. 有可能請你幫我嗎？
10. 你早上幾點開始工作？

Track 033

1. Have you read this article in the newspaper?
2. Do you know anyone called John?
3. Is the equipment ready?
4. Do you use English frequently in your job?
5. Do you think you could take the minutes?
6. Could you call Tracy for me?
7. Why do you want to learn English?
8. Who is your hero in the business world?
9. When did you first start working?
10. What are your plans for your career?

【中譯】

1. 你看過報上這篇文章了嗎？
2. 你有認識叫 John 的嗎？

3. 設備準備好了嗎？
4. 你在工作上經常使用英文嗎？
5. 你想你可以做會議記錄嗎？
6. 你可不可以幫我打電話給 Tracy ？
7. 你為什麼想學英文？
8. 商場上誰是你心目中的英雄？
9. 你最早是什麼時候開始工作的？
10. 你的職涯計畫是什麼？

Track 034

（Steve ：英國口音）

Mike: So let's talk about the figures on page 7 of the handout. Has everyone got a copy?

Macey: Yes.

Steve: I've got it.

Mike: Let's talk about the loss in the third quarter. Why is revenue down in that quarter?

Macey: Well, it's kind of hard to say. There are lots of factors.

Mike: What are the main factors?

Macey: Pardon me?

Mike: What are the main factors?

Macey: Well, the market has been very difficult, for one thing. Consumer spending was also down during that period. Also we were a salesperson short, as Mary was away on extended leave.

Mike: I see. Did you find anyone to replace her?

Macey: Well, no, it's hard to replace a salesperson temporarily.

Mike: I see. OK. Who was the best-performing salesperson during that period?

Macey: Sorry, you mean ...?

Mike: During that period, which of our sales team had the best results?

Macey: Oh well, you know, um … It was Lawrence Chou.

Mike: Is he getting a bonus?

Macey: Yes, he should, right?

Mike: Yes, he should. Could you let him know?

Macey: Sure. It will be my pleasure.

Mike: OK. Another question I have is about the costs. I see that costs rose during the same period. What was the main cost?

Steve: It was transportation costs.

Mike: Was that due to the price of oil?

Steve: Probably, yes. Shipping costs have also gone up.

Mike: Would it be possible for you to let me have a breakdown of our costs?

Steve: Sure. I'll get them to you later today.

Mike: Thanks.

【中譯】

Mike: 好，讓我們來談談講義第 7 頁上的數字。每個人都有一份嗎？

Macey: 有。

Steve: 我有拿到。

Mike: 我們來談談第三季的虧損情況。為什麼那一季的盈利下降？

Macey: 呃，這有點難說。有很多因素。

Mike: 主要因素是什麼？

Macey: 不好意思，你可以再說一遍嗎？

Mike: 主要因素是什麼？

Macey: 呃，市場不景氣，這是其一。那段時間顧客的消費力也降低了，還有我們少了一位業務員，因為 Mary 還在續假。

Mike: 我懂了。妳有找到人代她的班嗎？

Macey: 呃，沒有，很難找到短期的業務員。

Mike: 我懂了。好。誰是那一季當中表現最好的業務員？

Macey: 對不起，你是說……？

Mike: 那一季當中，我們的業務團隊誰的業績最好？

Macey: 哦，呃，你知道，嗯……是 Lawrence Chou 。

Mike: 他會拿到獎金嗎？

Macey: 會，他應該得的，對吧？

Mike: 對，是他該得的。妳可不可以告知他？

Macey: 沒問題。我很樂意。

Mike: 好。我還有另一個關於支出成本的問題。我看到同一季的支出成本也增加了，主要的成本項目是什麼呢？

Steve: 是交通費的成本。

Mike: 是因為油價的關係嗎？

Steve: 可能是。運輸費用也提高了。

Mike: 能不能請你把我們的支出成本明細列給我？

Steve: 沒問題，我今天稍晚就把明細拿給你。

Mike: 謝謝。

Unit 7

Please Don't Interrupt.

請不要打岔。

學習重點 聽出關鍵字和語調，讓你更有禮貌！

聽聽看

1 Sally、Tim 和 Jon 正在開會，請聽他們的會議對談，你可以聽懂多少？接著再聽一遍，這一次請在下方表格的正確欄位中打勾。 Track 035

		True	False
1	當地市場不景氣。		
2	顧客消費力提高。		
3	失業率下降。		
4	營業經理一直病得很嚴重。		
5	他們很快就找人接替營業經理了。		
6	工廠的新機器運作相當良好。		
7	Jon 一直打斷 Sally。		
8	Tim 沒有打斷 Sally。		
9	Jon 不喜歡 Sally。		

答案 請見 125 頁。CD 內容請見 127 頁。

你是否覺得最後一個問題很難回答。Sally 可能認為 Jon 不喜歡她，或是覺得他很無禮。她之所以會有這樣的感覺，是因為 Jon 一直打斷她的發言。這樣的行為總是會給人負面印象。但另一方面來說，這也可能只是 Jon 不知道什麼時候才是打斷發言的適當時機，或是聽不出來 Sally 是否已完整表達她的想法。事實上，他可能喜歡並且尊重 Sally，不是故意表現無禮。在時機適當時再打斷別人的發言，這一點很重要，如果你不能做到，就可能會留下負面印象。

在這個單元，我希望能夠讓各位聽出來，在英文中什麼時候才是打斷發言的適當時機。

一般通則是，你必須等到句子結束之後再打斷發言。句子結束就是想法表達完成，沒有人喜歡在想法完整表達之前被打斷。要聽出句子的結尾，你必須留意兩部分：

- 第一，說話者如何鋪陳他們的發言。
- 第二，說話者的語調。

讓我們先來練習第一部分。鋪陳發言的方法通常是使用一些指示字，例如：first、second、now、another thing、but、however 等等。聽出這些指示字，可以幫助你聽出句子的結尾。

動動腦

2 請看下列句子，在你認為是打斷發言的適當地方畫上斜線。

1. First, we need to reduce our spending. Second, we need to increase our sales.
2. It is not easy to increase sales. It's a slow market right now, and also, our products are kind of expensive.
3. This product is very good. It's cheap. Another thing I like about it is the size. It's small and easy to carry around.
4. Let's look at the figures in more detail. Please turn to page 7. You can see the figures for last year are pretty good. However, if you look at the figures for the first half of this year, you can see they are not so good.
5. The factory is working hard to complete this order on time. However, we are running out of materials. Also, the purchasing department is not helping us.

答案 請見 125 頁。注意，斜線總是出現在句子結束的地方，不是在句子中間。

現在，我們來練習語調。一般而言，句子要結束的時候，聲調會降低，語調下降。這即爲句子結束、也就是想法表達完成的信號。如果他們不想被打斷，語調會上揚，或是保持在一樣的聲調。

聽聽看 **3** 請聽 CD 播放的句子。注意語調。 Track 036

分析

- 留意聽發言者在句子結束時如何降低聲調。
- 留意聽發言者如何提高聲調；或是在 first 、 second 、 another thing 等指示字後面如何保持相同聲調。
- 如果你不能清楚聽出語調變化，請重複多聽幾遍。如有需要，可對照章末的 CD 內容。

另一個說話者鋪陳發言的方法是利用起頭字串，例如： There are a number of reasons why we should ...，然後再一一說明理由。你不可以在起頭字串和接續的句子之間打斷發言，不過在接下來的每一個句子之間你都可以插話。

動動腦 **4** 請看下列發言，在起頭字串下方畫底線，並在你認為可以打斷發言的地方畫上斜線。

1. There are three main problems here. First, the cost. Second, the delivery. And third, the quality.

2. There are a number of reasons why we should be careful. First, we don't know what our competitors are doing. Second, we might get it wrong.

3. Let's look at a few examples in more detail. Here you can see the figures for last year. And here, we can compare these figures with those of our competitors.

4. There are a number of issues we need to consider. First, are we doing the right thing? Second, what's it going to cost? And third, can we think of anything better?

5. Why do I think this? Let me explain. First, other companies have tried the same thing and not succeeded. Secondly, it's going to be expensive.

答案 請見 125 頁。

聽聽看 **5 請聽 CD 播放的句子，並注意語調。** Track 037

分析

- 留意發言者在句子結束時如何降低聲調。
- 如果你不能清楚聽出語調變化，請多聽幾遍。如有需要，可以對照章末的 CD 內容。

另外一個不應該打斷發言的地方，是當說話者在列舉項目的時候。做完下一個「動動腦」，你就會明白我所指爲何。

動動腦 6 請看下列發言，在你認為可以打斷發言的地方畫上斜線。

1. This product also comes in green, blue, red, and yellow.
2. We have branch offices in Bangkok, Taipei, Singapore, Tokyo, and Seattle.
3. Sales were down in February, March, April, and also May.
4. The leading chip producers are SMIC, UMC, and TSMC.
5. We need to order more scanners, monitors, printers, and keyboards.

答案 請見 126 頁。發現了嗎？你只能在項目列舉完畢後再發言。

聽聽看 7 請聽 CD 播放的句子，並注意語調。 Track 038

分析

- 留意聽發言者如何在列舉每一個項目之後提高聲調，然後在結束列舉時降低聲調。
- 如果你不能清楚聽出語調變化，請重複多聽幾遍。如有需要，可對照章末的 CD 內容。

接著我們來學一些打岔字串，讓你在打斷別人時可以更得體。

說說看

8 請研讀下列字串，並跟著 CD 練習把它們說得道地。 Track 039

打岔字串

- Sorry to interrupt, but … 不好意思打斷你，不過……
- Can I add something? 我可以補充一下嗎？
- Excuse me for interrupting, but … 不好意思打岔，不過……
- I don't mean to interrupt, but … 我不是故意打岔，不過……
- May I come in here? 我可以在這裡打斷一下嗎？
- May I interrupt you for a moment? 我可以打斷你一下嗎？
- I'd like to add something here if I may.
  如果可以，我想在這裡補充一些東西。

想要更熟悉打岔字串的用法，可以回頭聽聽 Track 035，留意這些字串如何在對談中使用。接下來，我們就來練習如何「說」這些字串。

說說看

9 請再把這些句子聽一遍，並在適當的地方暫停播放 CD，練習利用先前學到的打岔字串來打斷發言。

Track 036 Track 037 Track 038

聽聽看

10 請聽 Sarah、Tom 和 Jim 之間的會議對談。你認為誰在打岔時比較得體，Sarah 還是 Jim？為什麼？請專注在本章所學到的重點。 Track 040

分 析

- Jim 在打岔時比較得體，因為他遵守了我們所學過的原則。
- Sarah 在 Tom 列舉項目時打斷他兩次。（她的頭兩次打斷發言。）
- Sarah 在 Tom 使用起頭字串和接續的句子之間打斷他。（她的第三次打斷發言。）
- Sarah 在 Tom 使用指示字 Another thing 之後馬上打斷他。（她的第四次打斷發言。）
- 如果你沒聽出上述情況，請再聽一遍，如果需要，可以參考本章末的 CD 內容。

解答

聽聽看 1

1. **True.** 當地市場不景氣。
2. **False.** 顧客消費力下降。
3. **False.** 失業率上升。
4. **False.** 營業經理有小孩了。
5. **False.** 他們還沒有找人接替營業經理。
6. **False.** 他們工廠的新機器設備經常故障。
7. **True.** Jon 一直打斷 Sally。
8. **True.** Tim 沒有打斷 Sally。他在她說完話的時候才問她問題或提出看法。
9. 這個問題我們無法判斷。

動動腦 2

1. First, we need to reduce our spending. / Second, we need to increase our sales. /
2. It is not easy to increase sales. / It's a slow market right now, and also, our products are kind of expensive. /
3. This product is very good. / It's cheap. / Another thing I like about it is the size. / It's small and easy to carry around. /
4. Let's look at the figures in more detail. Please turn to page 7. You can see the figures for last year are pretty good. / However, if you look at the figures for the first half of this year, you can see they are not so good. /
5. The factory is working hard to complete this order on time. / However, we are running out of materials. / Also, the purchasing department is not helping us. /

動動腦 4

1. There are three main problems here. First, the cost. / Second, the

delivery. / And third, the quality. /

2. There are a number of reasons why we should be careful. First, we don't know what our competitors are doing. / Second, we might get it wrong. /
3. Let's look at a few examples in more detail. Here you can see the figures for last year. / And here, we can compare these figures with those of our competitors. /
4. There are a number of issues we need to consider. First, are we doing the right thing? / Second, what's it going to cost? / And third, can we think of anything better? /
5. Why do I think this? Let me explain. First, other companies have tried the same thing and not succeeded. / Secondly, it's going to be expensive. /

動動腦 6

1. This product also comes in green, blue, red, and yellow. /
2. We have branch offices in Bangkok, Taipei, Singapore, Tokyo, and Seattle. /
3. Sales were down in February, March, April, and also May. /
4. The leading chip producers are SMIC, UMC, and TSMC. /
5. We need to order more scanners, monitors, printers, and keyboards. /

CD 內容

Track 035

（Jon ：英國口音）

Tim: I'd like to ask Sally to brief us on the situation at her branch now.

Sally: Thanks, Tim. Well, things are not so good for a number of reasons. The first ...

Jon: Sorry to interrupt, but why is that Sally?

Sally: Mmm, the first is because the local economy is in a recession. This has of course affected consumer spending and ...

Jon: What about unemployment?

Sally: And unemployment is increasing all the time, with major lay offs every week. The second reason is that ...

Jon: Wow, that's bad.

Sally: The second reason is that we have been having problems at the branch itself.

Tim: I don't mean to interrupt, but what kind of problems?

Sally: Well, our operations manager left last month to go have a baby, and ...

Jon: A baby! How cute!

Sally: ... and it's been difficult to find anybody with the right kind of experience to replace her. We are still looking.

Tim: Can I add something? It's very difficult to find qualified and experienced people right now, even though unemployment is high. Most experienced people have already left to work in China.

Sally: Right. Another problem we've had ...

Jon: Sounds like you guys are having a tough time down there.

Sally: Yes, another problem we've had has been the machinery in the factory. It's old and breaks down a lot. Really it should be replaced, but ...

Jon: Yes, I agree.

Sally: However, I know we don't have the capital for ...

Jon: Yes, no money!

Sally: ... for this kind of investment.

【中譯】

Tim: 我現在想請Sally針對分公司的狀況為我們做個簡短的報告。

Sally: 謝謝，Tim。呃，狀況不甚理想的原因有幾點。首先……

Jon: 抱歉打斷一下，可是為什麼會這樣，Sally？

Sally: 嗯……首先是因為當地經濟不景氣。這當然影響了顧客的消費力和……

Jon: 那失業率呢？

Sally: 而且失業率一直在攀升，每星期都有大批的裁員。第二個原因是……

Jon: 哇，那很糟喔。

Sally: 第二個原因是我們分公司本身一直存在的問題。

Tim: 不是我要打岔，不過是哪一種問題呢？

Sally: 呃，我們的營業經理上個月離職去生小孩，而……

Jon: 小孩！真可愛！

Sally: ……而且一直很難找到經驗資格符合的人來接替她。我們還在找。

Tim: 我可以補充一下嗎？即使失業率很高，現在還是很難找到資格符合和有經驗的人。最有經驗的人都到中國去工作了。

Sally: 對。另外我們一直有一個問題……

Jon: 聽起來你們大夥兒在那裡處境很困難喔。

Sally: 是，另外我們一直存在的問題是工廠的機器設備，老舊又常故障，應該要淘汰換新，可是……

Jon: 是啊，我同意。

Sally: 可是，我知道我們沒有資金來……

Jon: 對，沒錢！

Sally: ……來做這方面的投資。

Track 036

1. First, we need to reduce our spending. Second, we need to increase our sales.
2. It is not easy to increase sales. It's a slow market right now, and also, our products are kind of expensive.
3. This product is very good. It's cheap. Another thing I like about it is the size. It's small and easy to carry around.
4. Let's look at the figures in more detail. Please turn to page 7. You can see the figures for last year are pretty good. However, if you look at the figures for the first half of this year, you can see they are not so good.
5. The factory is working hard to complete this order on time. However, we are running out of materials. Also, the purchasing department is not helping us.

【中譯】

1. 首先，我們必須減少支出。其次，我們必須提高業績。
2. 提高業績並不容易。現在的市場萎靡，而且，我們的產品又有點貴。
3. 這項產品非常好。很便宜。另外一點我喜歡的就是它的尺寸，小小的方便攜帶。
4. 讓我們更仔細來看看這些數字。請翻到第 7 頁。各位可以看到去年的數字相當亮眼，可是，如果你再看看今年上半年的數字，就會發現並不是那麼好。

5. 工廠方面正在努力如期完成這筆訂單。不過，我們的原料已經用完。而且，採購部門又不幫忙。

Track 037

1. There are three main problems here. First, the cost. Second, the delivery. And third, the quality.
2. There are a number of reasons why we should be careful. First, we don't know what our competitors are doing. Second, we might get it wrong.
3. Let's look at a few examples in more detail. Here you can see the figures for last year. And here, we can compare these figures with those of our competitors.
4. There are a number of issues we need to consider. First, are we doing the right thing? Second, what's it going to cost? And third, can we think of anything better?
5. Why do I think this? Let me explain. First, other companies have tried the same thing and not succeeded. Secondly, it's going to be expensive.

【中譯】

1. 這裡有三個主要問題。第一，成本。第二，送貨。還有第三，品質。
2. 我們必須謹慎的原因有幾個：第一，我們不知道競爭對手在做什麼。第二，我們可能搞錯了。
3. 讓我們更仔細地來看看一些例子。這裡各位可以看到去年的數字，還有這裡，我們可以把這些數字和競爭對手的數字做比較。
4. 有幾個問題我們必須考慮。第一，我們這樣做對嗎？第二，這會耗費多少成本？還有第三，我們可以想出更好的作法嗎？

5. 我為什麼這麼想？讓我來說明一下。首先，其他公司已經試過相同方式但並沒有成功。其次，這麼做的成本很高。

Track 038

1. This product also comes in green, blue, red, and yellow.
2. We have branch offices in Bangkok, Taipei, Singapore, Tokyo, and Seattle.
3. Sales were down in February, March, April, and also May.
4. The leading chip producers are SMIC, UMC, and TSMC.
5. We need to order more scanners, monitors, printers, and keyboards.

【中譯】

1. 這個產品還有綠色、藍色、紅色和黃色。
2. 我們有分公司在曼谷、台北、新加坡、東京和西雅圖。
3. 二月、三月、四月、還有五月的業績下滑。
4. 晶片製造商龍頭有 SMIC 、 UMC 和 TSMC 。
5. 我們必須訂購更多掃描器、螢幕、列印機和鍵盤。

Track 040

（Jim ：英國口音）

Tom: OK, let's look at this product in more detail. It comes in four sizes, small …

Sarah: Oh, I think that's too small.

Tom: … medium, large, and extra large.

Jim: Sorry to interrupt, but I think large is probably best for us. What colors do they have?

Tom: They have … let me see … five colors, green, red …

Sarah: Oh, I like the red best definitely!

Tom: … blue, yellow, and pink.

Jim: Yes, I like the red too. What do you think?

Tom: Well, I think we should choose the medium blue one for a number of reasons.

Sarah: Really? Why?

Tom: Well, first, I think blue would sell more units. Blue is the color that most people like, so it will be more popular.

Jim: Oh yes, good point. I'd like to add something here if I may. In our market research we found that blue is the color most people buy at this time of year.

Tom: Really? That's interesting, isn't it?

Jim: Yes, I thought so.

Tom: Another thing …

Sarah: Tom, don't you think the medium is too large for our customers?

Tom: No, I don't. Look, it fits these models here, and they are about the same size as our customers.

Sarah: Oh yes, you're right.

Tom: Also, medium is the same size as the other medium we sold last year, and we sold lots of those.

Jim: Can I add something?

Tom: Sure.

Jim: Medium is the most popular size of the other jackets we carry in the stores.

Tom: Oh, OK. Well, there you go.

【中譯】

Tom: 好，我們更仔細地來看看這項產品。它有四種尺寸，小號……

Sarah: 噢，我覺得那太小了。

Tom: 中號、大號和特大號。

Jim: 對不起打斷你，可是我覺得大號的可能最適合我們。他們有什麼顏色？

Tom: 他們有……我看看……五種顏色，綠色、紅色……

Sarah: 哦，我最愛紅色了！

Tom: ……藍色、黃色和粉紅色。

Jim: 對，我也喜歡紅色。你覺得呢？

Tom: 呃，基於幾個理由，我想我們應該選擇藍色中號的。

Sarah: 真的嗎？為什麼？

Tom: 呃，首先，我認為藍色會賣得比較好。藍色是大部分人都喜歡的顏色，所以會比較受歡迎。

Jim: 沒錯，有道理。如果可以，我想補充一下。在我們的市場調查中，我們發現藍色是年度這個時期大多數人所買的顏色。

Tom: 真的嗎？這很有意思，不是嗎？

Jim: 是的，我也這麼覺得。

Tom: 另外……

Sarah: Tom，你不覺得中號對我們顧客來說太大了嗎？

Tom: 不，我不覺得。你看，對這些人型模特兒來說都很合身，它們和我們消費客群的尺寸差不多。

Sarah: 喔對，你說的沒錯。

Tom: 還有，中號和我們去年賣的中號尺寸一樣，而且我們賣了很多。

Jim: 我可以補充一下嗎？

Tom: 當然。

Jim: 中號是我們店面賣的其他夾克最受歡迎的尺寸。

Tom: 哦，好，嗯，這就對了。

Unit 8

That's Not What I Meant.

那不是我的意思。

學習重點 重音，釐清誤會就靠它！

聽聽看

1 Steve 和 Mary 正在開會。請聽他們的會議對談，你可以聽懂多少？接著再聽一遍，並在下列表格的正確欄位打勾。 Track 041

		True	False
1	專案進度正常。		
2	業績萎縮 2%。		
3	信貸緊縮影響了業績。		
4	目前的主要市場是日本。		
5	歐洲業績下滑。		

答案 請見 142 頁。

在這場會議中，你可以聽到與會者誤解彼此意思的狀況，以及他們更正訊息的方式。

句子中單字的重讀方式可能會改變一個句子的意思。而一個句子也可能因爲單字重讀的方式不同，而有許多不同意思。舉例說明如下：

John told me that the XY project was behind schedule.

John 告訴我，XY 專案的進度落後。

根據所要表達的意思，這個句子可以有五種不同的重讀方式。如果用平鋪直述的方式說這個句子，不特別重讀某個字，那麼，句子單純就是它本身的意思而已。不過，如果對方誤以爲這個訊息是由 Mike 所告知，那麼重讀 John 這個字，就表示告知訊息的人是 John，而非 Mike。能夠聽出重讀字和解讀背後涵義非常重要，因爲這是在英文中釐清誤解的主要方法。在本單元，我們會加強你聽出此類「對照重音」的能力。

動動腦

2 在下列句子中，粗體字表示重讀的部分。重讀的方式不同，它們所要傳達的意義分別為何？請將句子的號碼寫在正確意義的欄位前。請看範例。

1. **John** told me that the XY project was behind schedule.
2. John **told** me that the XY project was behind schedule.
3. John told **me** that the XY project was behind schedule.
4. John told me that the **XY** project was behind schedule.
5. John told me that the XY **project** was behind schedule.
6. John told me that the XY project was **behind** schedule.

	He was talking about the XY project, not the AB project.
	John said it was behind schedule, not ahead of schedule.
	John didn't tell Lucy — he told me.
	John told me — he didn't write to me.
	John wasn't talking about the XY product — he was talking about the XY project.
1	It was John who told me, not David.

答案 請見 142 頁。

聽聽看

3 現在請聽上一題的句子，第一遍沒有強調特定的字。確定你可以聽出重音的不同之後，請跟著覆誦，練習使用重音來傳達不同意思。 Track 042

4 請看下列句子和它們所要傳達的意義。根據所要表達的意義，將你認為應該重讀的字畫上底線。

動動腦

1. Mike went to the U.S. last week for a few days on business.
   → **He went on business, not for a vacation.**

2. Mike went to the U.S. last week for a few days on business.
   → **He went last week, not yesterday.**

3. Mike went to the U.S. last week for a few days on business.
   → **He went to the U.S., not the U.K.**

4. Mike went to the U.S. last week for a few days on business.
   → **He was only gone for a few days, not a few weeks.**

5. Mike went to the U.S. last week for a few days on business.
   → **It was Mike who went, not John.**

答案 請見142頁。核對完答案，請聽 Track 043 並跟著覆誦，練習使用重音來傳達不同意思。

好，你現在應該對重音的使用比較有概念了。接著就來測試一下，聽到句子時，你能否判讀出其所要表達的意思。

5 請聽 CD 播放的句子，並選出它們所要表達的意義。

聽聽看

Track 044

______ 1. Mary is my boss.

a. It's Mary who is my boss, not Julie.

b. She is my boss, I have to be careful what I say to her.

_____ **2.** Steve told me that the project is behind schedule.

a. The project is not on schedule.

b. It was Steve who told me, not Eugene.

_____ **3.** The client likes the color.

a. They don't like the size.

b. It's not correct to say they don't like the color.

_____ **4.** The ABC project is over budget.

a. It's this project which is over budget, not the other one.

b. It's over budget, not under budget.

_____ **5.** We need to complete this stage of the project before next month.

a. It's this stage we need to complete, not the other stage.

b. We need to finish it before next month, not during next month.

_____ **6.** The report says 23,000 units.

a. The correct number is 23,000, not 25,000.

b. The report is talking about units, not about points.

_____ **7.** Sales were up two points last month.

a. They were up, not down.

b. The amount was two points, not three points.

_____ **8.** The Taiwan market is very slow at the moment.

a. We think it will improve next year.

b. It's the Taiwan market I'm talking about, not another market.

答案 請見143頁。

好，接著我們來學一些釐清誤解的字串。

動動腦 6 請將下列字串分類填入正確的欄位。

- Are you sure?
- Is that right?
- That's not what I meant.
- No, hang on.
- Do you mean X or Y?
- No, X, not Y.

釐清	要求釐清

答案 請見143頁。核對完答案，請聽 Track 045，練習這些字串的說法。

想要更熟練這些字串的使用方式，可以回頭聽聽 Track 041，留意它們在對談中如何使用。如果需要，可以參考本章後面的 CD 內容。

聽聽看

7 現在請聽另一段會議對談，並在下表的正確欄位打勾。請專注在本單元學過的重點，看看你進步了多少。

Track 046

		True	False
1	獲利增加 2%。		
2	盈收與上一季相比增加了 2%。		
3	盈收與去年相比下滑。		
4	獲利全面增加。		
5	由於原物料成本增加，獲利減少。		

答案 請見 143 頁。

解答

聽聽看 1

1. **False.** 根據 John 所說，專案進度現在是落後的。
2. **False.** 業績萎縮了 5% 。
3. **False.** 影響業績的是石油價格上漲，並不是信貸緊縮。
4. **True.**
5. **False.** 歐洲的業績也提高了，只是不如日本那麼多。

動動腦 2

4	He was talking about the XY project, not the AB project.
6	John said it was behind schedule, not ahead of schedule.
3	John didn't tell Lucy — he told me.
2	John told me — he didn't write to me.
5	John wasn't talking about the XY product — he was talking about the XY project.
1	It was John who told me, not David.

動動腦 4

1. Mike went to the U.S. last week for a few days on business.
   ➜ 他是出差，不是度假。

2. Mike went to the U.S. last week for a few days on business.
   ➜ 他上星期去的，不是昨天。

3. Mike went to the U.S. last week for a few days on business.
   ➜ 他去美國，不是英國。

4. Mike went to the U.S. last week for a few days on business.
   ➜ 他只去幾天，不是幾個星期。

5. Mike went to the U.S. last week for a few days on business.
   ➜ 去的人是 Mike ，不是 John 。

聽聽看 5

1. a 2. b 3. b 4. b 5. a 6. a 7. a 8. b

動動腦 6

釐清	要求釐清
• **No, hang on.** 不對，等等。 • **No, X, not Y.** 不，是 X ，不是 Y 。 • **That's not what I meant.** 那不是我的意思。	• **Do you mean X or Y?** 你是指 X 還是 Y ？ • **Are you sure?** 你確定嗎？ • **Is that right?** 這樣對嗎？

聽聽看 7

1. **False.** 是盈收增加了 2% ，不是獲利。
2. **True.**
3. **True.**
4. **False.** 獲利全面減少。
5. **False.** 獲利減少是因為交通費用增加的緣故。

CD 內容

Track 041

Steve: So, what's happening?

Mary: Well, I spoke to John yesterday about the project.

Steve: Oh yes, and what did he say?

Mary: The project is behind schedule.

Steve: Oh, are you sure? I spoke to Mike a few days ago and he said it was on schedule.

Mary: Well, John said it was behind schedule now.

Steve: Oh. Something must have happened. And how are the sales in your region?

Mary: Oh sales have shrunk 5% due to the increase in oil prices.

Steve: Oh well 2% is not too bad.

Mary: No, 5%, not 2%.

Steve: And the credit crisis has affected everyone.

Mary: The increase in oil prices is responsible for our sales drop.

Steve: Oh. Well. What about our main market? Is it still Europe?

Mary: No, it's changed now. According to the new figures, the main market is now Japan.

Steve: European sales are down, and Japan is up? Is that right?

Mary: No, that's not what I meant. European sales are also up, but not as much as Japan. Japan has overtaken Europe.

Steve: Really? That's good news.

【中譯】

Steve: 嘿，怎麼了？

Mary: 呃，我昨天跟 John 談到這個專案。

Steve: 是喔，他怎麼說？

Mary: 專案進度落後了。

Steve: 噢，妳確定嗎？我前幾天跟 Mike 談過，他說進度正常呀。

Mary: 呃， John 說目前進度落後。

Steve: 噢，一定發生了什麼事。還有妳那個地區的業績如何？

Mary: 噢，業績萎縮了 5% ，因為石油價格上漲的緣故。

Steve: 唔， 2% 還不算太糟。

Mary: 不對，是 5% ，不是 2% 。

Steve: 而且信貸危機對每個人都有影響。

Mary: 石油價格上漲是造成我們業績下滑的原因。

Steve: 好吧。那我們的主要市場呢？還是歐洲嗎？

Mary: 不，現在不一樣了。根據新數字顯示，現在的主要市場是日本。

Steve: 歐洲的業績下滑，而日本卻提高了？是嗎？

Mary: 不，我不是那個意思。歐洲業績也提高了，只是沒有日本那麼多。日本已經超越歐洲了。

Steve: 真的？那可是好消息。

Track 044

1. **Mary** is my boss.
2. **Steve** told me that the project is behind schedule.
3. The client **likes** the color.
4. The ABC project is **over** budget.
5. We need to complete **this** stage of the project before next month.
6. The report says **23,000** units.
7. Sales were **up** two points last month.
8. The **Taiwan** market is very slow at the moment.

【中譯】

1. Mary 是我的上司。
2. Steve 告訴我這個專案的進度落後。
3. 客戶喜歡這個顏色。
4. ABC 專案超出預算。
5. 我們必須在下個月之前完成專案的這個階段。
6. 報告上說有 23,000 個單位。
7. 上個月的業績提高了兩個百分點。
8. 現階段台灣的市場成長緩慢。

Track 046

Steve: OK, let's talk about the report. In the report it says that profits were up 2%, but yesterday, Jackie told me they were down. Is that right?

Mary: No, hang on, I think she means they were up 2% compared with the previous quarter, but down compared with the same time last year.

Steve: Oh OK, yes that makes sense.

Mary: And I think she means revenues were up. In the report it says revenues. Profits were down all over due to rising transportation costs.

Steve: Do you mean profits or revenues?

Mary: Revenues.

Steve: So revenues are up 2% compared with the previous quarter, but down compared with the same time last year.

Mary: Yes, that's right.

Steve: And the reason is rising raw materials costs.

Mary: That's not what I meant. Rising transportation costs.

Steve: Oh, OK. I got it.

【中譯】

Steve: 好，我們來談談這份報告。報告中指出獲利增加了 2% ，可是昨天 Jackie 告訴我獲利減少了。對嗎？

Mary: 不，等一下。我想她的意思是跟上一季相比增加了 2% ，可是跟去年同期相比則是減少。

Steve: 喔好，這樣說有道理。

Mary: 而且我想她指的是盈收增加。在報告中指的是盈收，獲利則是全面減少，因為運輸成本增加的緣故。

Steve: 你是指獲利還是盈收？

Mary: 盈收。

Steve: 所以盈收跟上一季相比增加了 2% ，可是跟去年同期相比卻減少。

Mary: 是，沒錯。

Steve: 而原因是原物料費用上漲。

Mary: 我不是那個意思。是運輸成本增加。

Steve: 喔好，我懂了。

Unit 9

You Say Tomato, I Say Tomato.

你說蕃茄，我說蕃茄。

學習重點 美式、英式，雙聲都會通！

聽聽看 **1** Janet 在一家精品公司上班，她正在會議上作簡介，你能聽懂她說了些什麼嗎？接著再聽一遍，並在下表的正確欄位上打勾。 Track 047

		True	False
1	奢侈品市場未受影響。		
2	股市變得不穩定。		
3	有錢人收入減少、消費力降低。		
4	消費者負擔不起奢侈品。		
5	人們對於花費不是很謹慎。		

答案 請見 156 頁。如果你無法完全理解所聽到的內容，可以參閱本章末的 CD 內容。

在上一場會議中，Janet 說的是美式發音。我們接著來聽聽 John 所作的簡介，他說的則是英式發音。

聽聽看 **2** 請聽 John 所作的相同簡介。你可以聽出他和 Janet 的發音哪裡不同嗎？ Track 048

美式英語和英式英語之間有諸多差異。一如美式英語本身即有各種不同口音，英式英語亦是如此。大多數亞洲國家學習的都是美式英語，不過新加坡、香港和泰國學習的是英式英語。

在這個單元中，要帶領各位認識美式和英式英語之間的一些差異，進而幫助你們理解英式英語。讓各位在面對說話帶英國腔的客戶時，也能從容應對。

美式和英式發音的基本差異有三點：

1. 英式英語的子音通常發音比較清楚。
2. 英式英語的 "r" 在母音之後通常不發音。
3. 英式英語的母音發音和美式有些不同。

我們接著來進一步討論這三點差異。

❶ **英式英語的子音通常發音比較清楚**，尤其是多音節單字中的字母 "t"，在美式英語中這個字母有時會軟化發音為 /d/，在英式英語中則清楚地發音為 /t/。

聽聽看 **3** 美式、英式發音比一比，你會先聽到單字的美式發音，接著是英式發音。 Track 049

■ ability	■ possibility
■ artificial	■ productivity
■ audited	■ profitability
■ capability	■ responsibility
■ committed	■ strategy
■ environmental	■ totally

說說看 **4** 能夠聽出其中差異後，這一次請跟著 CD 覆誦，熟練美式、英式的不同唸法。 Track 049

❷ **英式英語的 "r" 在母音之後通常不發音**。反之，如果 "r" 屬於單字中母音的一部分，則會加長發音，如： girl ；若是 "r" 在字尾，則發音近似 /ə/，如： weather 。

聽聽看

5 美式、英式發音比一比，你會先聽到單字的美式發音，接著是英式發音。 Track 050

■ car	■ software
■ dollar	■ speaker
■ four	■ sure
■ more	■ there
■ prepare	■ word
■ purchase	■ work

聽聽看

6 能夠聽出其中差異後，這一次請跟著 CD 覆誦，熟練美式、英式的不同唸法。 Track 050

❸ **英式英語的母音發音和美式有些不同**，例如 hot 、 pot 和 half 、 past 中的母音發音，尤以後者差異最大。

聽聽看

7 美式、英式發音比一比，你會先聽到單字的美式發音，接著是英式發音。 Track 051

■ boss	■ got
■ cost	■ job
■ economy	■ lost

■ obvious	■ product
■ optional	■ technology
■ problem	■ probably

聽聽看

8 能夠聽出其中差異後，這一次請跟著 CD 覆誦，熟練美式、英式的不同唸法。 Track 051

我們接著來看看 half 和 past 的發音。美式英語的母音發音爲 /æ/；英式英語的母音發音則爲 /ɑ/。

聽聽看

9 美式、英式發音比一比，你會先聽到單字的美式發音，接著是英式發音。 Track 052

■ advance	■ enhance
■ after	■ France
■ answer	■ grant
■ ask	■ plant
■ can't	■ sample
■ chance	■ task

聽聽看

10 能夠聽出其中差異後，這一次請跟著 CD 覆誦，熟練美式、英式的不同唸法。 Track 052

熟悉了單字的發音差異，現在我們延伸到句子的學習。

聽聽看

11 請聽 CD 播放的句子，這些句子分別是美式還是英式口音？請在正確的欄位打勾。 Track 053

		U.S.	U.K.
1	We need to make sure we can totally enhance our technology.		
2	We currently don't have the ability to provide you with a sample software product.		
3	They audited us four months ago and we got a high safety score, but they still asked us to make some changes.		
4	The speaker did not give us a chance to ask questions about his strategy, so we lost the opportunity to hear more.		
5	We have a responsibility to prepare answers in case the boss asks questions.		
6	The obvious problem we're having with the plant in France was caused by the artificial environmental factors at work there.		
7	Productivity and profitability are high and we can buy more for our dollar. The economy is probably better too, more advanced after the change of government 10 years ago.		

答案 請見 156 頁。可以多聽幾遍，利用先前學到的重點來分辨差異。能夠聽出差異之後，再跟著 CD 覆誦，學習二種腔調的說法。

聽聽看

12 請再聽一次前面的句子，注意到了嗎，這一次的腔調不同了。請留意它們和前一個練習的發音差異。能夠聽出差異之後，也請跟著 CD 覆誦，練習不同腔調的說法。

Track 054

想要和外國客戶從容對談，只進展到單句的學習是不夠的，接著我們就來挑戰整個段落的聽力和口說吧。

聽聽看

13 請聽 Mary 在會議上所作的簡介。她在一家成衣公司任職，你能聽出她說了些什麼嗎？請在下表的正確欄位打勾。 Track 055

		True	False
1	她在談論成衣市場。		
2	主要通路是便利商店。		
3	她談到產品種類和對應的市場佔有率。		
4	男性服飾賣的比女性好。		
5	童裝未包含在簡介中。		
6	這個市場一直在成長，競爭也愈來愈激烈。		
7	市場上大部分的成衣都是奢侈品。		

答案 請見 156 頁。

聽聽看

14 請聽 Joseph 所作的相同簡介。聽出來了嗎？他說的是英國口音，聽的時候請專注在本章所學的重點，看看你進步了多少。 Track 056

解答

聽聽看 1

1. **False.** 它已經開始受到影響。
2. **True.**
3. **True.**
4. **True.**
5. **False.** 每個人對於消費都更加謹慎。

聽聽看 11

1. 美式	2. 英式	3. 英式	4. 美式
5. 英式	6. 英式	7. 美式	

聽聽看 13

1. **True.**
2. **False.** 主要的銷售通路是百貨公司。
3. **True.**
4. **False.** 女性服飾賣的比較好。
5. **False.** 兒童服飾也包含在簡介內。
6. **True.**
7. **False.** 市場上大多數的成衣產品都不是昂貴的品項。

CD 內容

Track 047 Track 048

I think the luxury goods market has begun to suffer already. Certainly the volatility in the stock markets and the great declines that we've seen have impacted even high-end consumers' ability to spend. The growing awareness of affordable luxury has definitely been called into question now because even those consumers don't have the same level of income as they once had. So whatever type of consumer you are, if your net worth is lower than what it had been before the stock market crash, it seems obvious that you will be more careful about your spending.

【中譯】

我認為奢侈品市場已經開始受到衝擊。我們所看到的股市震盪和經濟大衰退，肯定連金字塔頂端消費群的消費能力都受到影響。逐漸提升的平價奢侈品消費意識現在的確受到了質疑，因為連那些消費者的收入水平也不如以往。所以無論你是哪一類型的消費者，如果你的財產淨值低於股市崩盤之前，很顯然你對於你的支出就會更加謹慎。

Track 049

- ability 能力
- artificial 人造的；人工的
- audited 檢查；查帳
- capability 能力；性能
- committed 犯罪；投入（某事）
- environmental 環境的
- possibility 可能性
- productivity 生產力
- profitability 獲利能力
- responsibility 責任
- strategy 策略
- totally 全面地

Track 050

- car 汽車
- dollar（美）元
- four 四
- more 更多
- prepare 準備
- purchase 購買
- software 軟體
- speaker 演講者；說話者
- sure 確定的
- there 那裡
- word 字
- work 工作

Track 051

- boss 老闆；上司
- cost 成本
- economy 經濟
- got 得到（過去式）
- job 工作
- lost 失去（過去式）
- obvious 明顯的
- optional 可選擇的
- problem 問題
- product 產品
- technology 科技
- probably 可能地

Track 052

- advance 提升；增進
- after 之後
- answer 回答
- ask 問
- can't 不能
- chance 機會
- enhance 加強
- France 法國
- grant 許可；授與
- plant 工廠
- sample 樣本
- task 任務；工作

Track 053 Track 054

1. We need to make sure we can totally enhance our technology.

2. We currently don't have the ability to provide you with a sample software product.
3. They audited us four months ago, and we got a high safety score, but they still asked us to make some changes.
4. The speaker did not give us a chance to ask questions about his strategy, so we lost the opportunity to hear more.
5. We have a responsibility to prepare answers in case the boss asks questions.
6. The obvious problem we're having with the plant in France was caused by the artificial environmental factors at work there.
7. Productivity and profitability are high, and we can buy more for our dollar. The economy is probably better too, more advanced after the change of government ten years ago.

【中譯】

1. 我們必須確定我們可以全面提升我們的技術。
2. 我們目前沒有能力提供你軟體產品的樣本。
3. 他們四個月前來檢查，我們的安全措施獲得高分，不過他們還是要求我們做一些改變。
4. 演講人沒有給我們機會針對他的策略提出問題，所以我們錯失聽到更多的機會。
5. 我們有責任準備答案，以防老闆提出問題。
6. 我們在法國的工廠所遭遇的顯著問題，是當地工作上的人為環境因素所引起。
7. 生產力和獲利能力都很高，我們可以用我們的錢買到更多東西。經濟情況可能也變好了，在十年前的政府改造後更進步了。

Track 055 Track 056

OK, well, I just want to brief you all on the ready-to-wear market here in Taiwan. To start with, let's look at the character of the market. The main outlet for this kind of product is department stores, for instance, Sogo and Mitsukoshi. I would now like to turn briefly to the products. What kind of products are the most popular? Page 5 shows the range of products and the market share of each category. You can see that women's clothes are bigger sellers compared with men's clothes and children's clothes. What's more, the market has been growing for the last two years with more local products coming onto the market. This means that the market is getting more competitive. Most of the ready-to-wear products on the market are not luxury items, and note also that ...

【中譯】

好的，嗯，我只是想跟各位簡單報告一下台灣這裡的成衣市場。首先，我們來看看市場特性。這種產品的主要通路是百貨公司，例如 Sogo 和新光三越。現在我想再簡單談談產品部分。哪一類產品最暢銷？在第 5 頁可以看到產品分類和每一類的市場佔有率。各位可以看到女性服飾比男性服飾和兒童服飾賣的好。還有，它的市場在過去兩年也一直成長，有更多當地的產品上市。這表示它的市場競爭愈來愈激烈。大多數市場上的成衣產品都不是昂貴奢華的品項，而且注意……

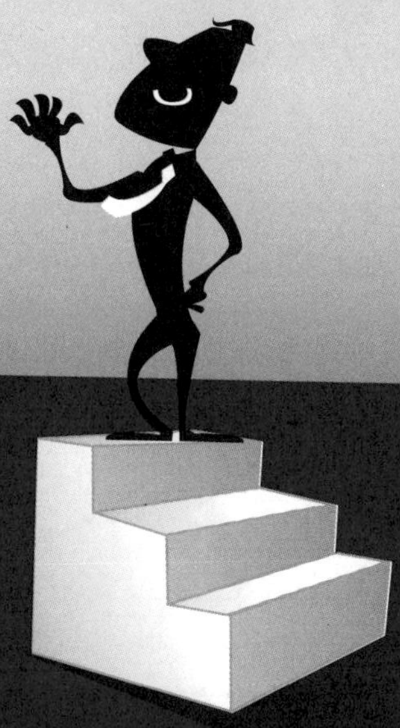

Part 3

電話篇

Telephoning

Unit 10

Is That 15 Or 50?

那是 15 還是 50 ？

學習重點 聽力剋星——數字——的征服攻略！

聽聽看 **1** Max 正在留言給 John 的秘書，你能夠聽懂多少呢？請再聽一遍，並完成下列表格。 Track 057

Max's Cell Phone	
Max's Landline	
Product Serial Number	
Project Deadline	
Call Back Time	
Bill Amount	

答案 請見 172 頁。

從電話對談中把數字訊息正確記下來，是件讓人頭痛的事，尤其是一連串的長數字。還好，有一些說長數字的原則可以學習，這些原則也可以幫助你聽懂它們。在上面這則對話中，我們聽到了 6 種數字：手機號碼、室內電話或傳真號碼、產品序號、日期、時間和金額。我們來看看這些不同的數字要怎麼唸。

電話號碼

- 電話號碼通常會切成三到四個數字一組，每一組絕對不會超過四個數字，也不會少於兩個。
- 手機號碼會切成三組，第一組有四個數字，第二組和第三組各有三個數字，例如：XXXX-XXX-XXX。
- 室內電話號碼通常會切成兩組，各是四個數字。其他國家的電話號碼則有其他模式。

唸電話號碼的模式通常為：每一組數字的最後一個字語調上揚，暫停，然後再降低語調開始唸下一組數字。完整電話號碼的最後一個字語調下降。

聽的時候注意這些上、下語調和停頓，可以幫助你把數字聽得更清楚、並把它們正確地記下來。我們接著就來練習看看。

聽聽看

2 請聽下列電話號碼，並注意語調。聽第二遍的時候請跟著覆誦，練習說電話號碼的語調模式。 Track 058

1. 0952 ↗ 636 ↗ 785 ↘
2. 0931 ↗ 973 ↗ 568 ↘
3. 0963 ↗ 859 ↗ 527 ↘
4. 2279 ↗ 6377 ↘
5. 2290 ↗ 6894 ↘
6. 8493 ↗ 9753 ↘

聽聽看

3 請聽 CD 播放的電話號碼並將它們記下來。 Track 059

1 ____________________

2 ____________________

3 ____________________

4 ____________________

5 ____________________

6 ____________________

7 ____________________

8 ____________________

9 ____________________

10 ____________________

答案 請見 172 頁。

產品序號

產品序號通常也會切成四個或三個數字一組，語調模式和電號碼相同：每一組數字的最後一個字語調上揚，暫停，然後降低語調開始下一組數字。唸產品序號和電話號碼時，必須注意幾件事情：

- 第一，美國人和英國人的唸法有一顯著差異：美國人通常會把 0 唸成 "zero"，而英國人通常會唸成 "oh"，我建議你把 0 唸成 "oh"，因爲發音比較簡單清楚。（如果英文和數字並列的字串，爲避免 oh 的發音和字母 o 搞混，可改把數字 0 唸成 zero）
- 第二，0007 此類數字，通常會這樣唸：double oh, oh seven 或 double zero, zero, seven。更長一點的序號，例如：00 00 088，則會這樣唸：double oh, double oh, oh, double eight 或 double zero, double zero, zero, double eight。幾乎沒有人會用 triple zero 來表示三個零，所以不要這麼說，否則對方可能會搞不清楚你在說些什麼。此類長數字的語調模式也是一樣：每一組數字的最後一個字語調上揚，然後在全部數字的最後一個字把語調下降。
- 第三，有一些序號會包括「點」（唸成 point）和「斜線」（唸成 slash）或「破折號」（唸成 dash）。

聽聽看

4 請聽下列序號，留意語調和停頓的方式。聽第二遍的時候請跟著覆誦，練習說序號的方法。 Track 060

1. 00 00 752 156
2. 2377 7739 41
3. AB55 8413
4. 555 792 15X

5. 99 66 33 123S

6. 00 00 00 55 AJ

聽聽看

5 請聽 CD 播放的產品序號並將它們寫下來。

Track 061

1 ______________ 6 ______________

2 ______________ 7 ______________

3 ______________ 8 ______________

4 ______________ 9 ______________

5 ______________ 10 ______________

答案 請見 172 頁。

日期

日期的英文說法有很多種方式。在美式英語中，通常會先說月份，如：August 25, 2010。在英式英語和大多數的歐洲國家，則是先說日期，如：25 August 2010。

聽聽看

6 請聽下列日期的唸法，聽熟之後，請跟著覆誦。

Track 062

1. August 26, 2010
2. 26 August 2010
3. 26.08.2010
4. 08-26, 2010

註 在唸日期時，必須以序數的方式來唸，如：August 3 必須唸成 August 3rd；而在書寫日期時，以數字呈現，寫成 August 3 即可。

聽聽看

7 請聽 CD 播放的日期，並將它們寫出來。

Track 063

1 ______________

2 ______________

3 ______________

4 ______________

5 ______________

6 ______________

答案 請見 172 頁。

時間

說時間的方式有三種：

1. 使用數字：six thirty（六點半）。
2. 使用單字和數字：half past six（六點半）。
3. 使用二十四小時制的數字表示，如：18:30（下午六點半）。這個方式在寫作上比較常見，較少在口語中使用，所以不太需要擔心它。

第一種方式最簡單：你只要把你聽到的數字記下來就可以。第二種方式，結合了單字和數字，就比較困難。我們來練習一下。

動動腦

8 連連看，請把左欄字串和它們所代表的時間配對。做完配對練習，可跟著 CD 覆誦，練習時間的說法。

Track 064

■ a quarter past x	•	•	x點
■ ten past x	•	•	x點5分
■ twenty past x	•	•	x點10分
■ five past x	•	•	x點15分
■ a quarter to x	•	•	x點20分
■ twenty to x	•	•	x點半
■ half past x	•	•	再20分x點
■ ten to x	•	•	再10分x點
■ five to x	•	•	再5分x點
■ x o' clock	•	•	再15分x點

答案 請見173頁。

分 析

- 注意，超過整點的前 30 分鐘，用 past 這個字來表示，如：ten past eight（八點十分）；後 30 分鐘，用「to + 下一個鐘點」，如：twenty to seven（再二十分鐘就七點了，即現在是六點四十分）。
- 注意，quarter 前面要加 "a"。
- 注意，使用下列二種表示方式時，「分」會放在「小時」前面，如：ten past eight（八點十分）或 a quarter to nine（八點四十五分）。

聽聽看

9 請聽 CD 播放的這些時間，把它們記下來。

Track 065

1 ____________________ 3 ____________________

2 ____________________ 4 ____________________

5 ____________　　8 ____________

6 ____________　　9 ____________

7 ____________　　10 ____________

答案 請見 173 頁。

數字

英文的長串數字是聽力一大挑戰。下列有三個唸數字的基本原則：

1. 數字是由左至右唸出，但所有的數字從右邊開始每三個數字切成一組。如： 123 會唸成 one hundred and twenty-three ； 1,234 會唸成 one thousand, two hundred and thirty-four ； 12,345 則會唸成 twelve thousand, three hundred and forty-five 。
2. 如果數字裡有百位和十位、個位數，就會用 hundred and 來表示。如： 3,750 會唸成 three thousand, seven hundred and fifty 。
3. Million 或 billion 等字，都不用加 s 。

說說看 **10** 請練習說下列數字。

- 123
- 1,234
- 12,345
- 123,456
- 1,234,567
- 12,345,678
- 123,456,789
- 1,234,567,890

答案 請聽 Track 066，你唸對了嗎，如果沒有，請跟著 CD 多練習幾次。

聽聽看 **11** 請把你聽到的數字寫下來。 Track 067

1 ______________ 6 ______________

2 ______________ 7 ______________

3 ______________ 8 ______________

4 ______________ 9 ______________

5 ______________ 10 ______________

答案 請見 173 頁。

聽聽看 **12** 現在請聽另一段電話對談，聽的時候請一邊完成下列表格。請專注在本單元所學到的重點，看看你進步了多少。 Track 068

Susan's Cell Phone	
Susan's Landline	
Train Time	
Correct Bill Amount	
Wrong Bill Amount	
Product Serial Number	
Project Deadline	

答案 請見 174 頁。

解答

聽聽看 1

Max's Cell Phone	0953 125 487
Max's Landline	2274 7642 Extension 274
Product Serial Number	00027405X2
Project Deadline	13.3.2010
Call Back Time	4:30
Bill Amount	$123,759, $275,264

聽聽看 3

1. 0963 148 637
2. 2285 8995
3. 0582 175 739
4. 886 3286 0895
5. 0963 274 973
6. 41 2276 7743 787
7. 0952 783 159
8. 85 254 7789 653
9. 0963 129 852
10. 2285 0007

聽聽看 5

1. ISBN 9577295894
2. Abd 006 386
3. Version 10 4 11-A
4. 55 55 5892
5. 7524.796
6. ABX33.777
7. 55 55 55
8. 147-2357.8
9. Unit 567 89 5
10. AY147.700

聽聽看 7

1. 2006 年 7 月 15 日
2. 2009 年 12 月 25 日
3. 1973 年 8 月 9 日
4. 2000 年 1 月 10 日
5. 2000 年 3 月 11 日
6. 1997 年 9 月 15 日

動動腦 8

a quarter past x	x點15分
ten past x	x點10分
twenty past x	x點20分
five past x	x點5分
a quarter to x	再15分x點
twenty to x	再20分x點
half past x	x點30分
ten to x	再10分x點
five to x	再5分x點
x o' clock	x點

聽聽看 9

1. **2:00**
2. **4:40**
3. **12:10**
4. **6:45**
5. **3:20**
6. **6:30**
7. **11:05**
8. **8:50**
9. **1:55**
10. **4:15**

聽聽看 11

1. **163**
2. **1,784**
3. **84,832**
4. **965,425**
5. **8,532,185**
6. **95,642,734**
7. **8,675**
8. **946,723**
9. **12,000**
10. **57,931**

聽聽看 12

Susan's Cell Phone	0953 285 684
Susan's Landline	02 2678 6543 extension 678
Train Time	7:05a.m.
Correct Bill Amount	$234,678
Wrong Bill Amount	$2,346,788
Product Serial Number	XYW550007
Project Deadline	4.04.2009

CD 內容

Track 057

Max: Hi. Can I speak to John, please?

Mary: Oh, I'm sorry, John's in a meeting at the moment.

Max: Oh. When will he be free? I have to speak to him very urgently.

Mary: Mmm, not sure. Can I take a message?

Max: OK, can you tell him that Max called?

Mary: Max, OK. Does he have your number?

Max: No. Can I give you my mobile?

Mary: Sure, go ahead.

Max: It's 0953-125-487.

Mary: 0953-125-487.

Max: That's correct. And my landline is 2274-7642, extension 274.

Mary: Sorry, can you repeat that?

Max: 2274-7642, extension 274. Got it?

Mary: Yes.

Max: OK, now please tell him that we are having problems at the factory with the specs for the product with the serial number 00027405X2. We cannot proceed until he clarifies the specs for us. The project is already delayed and the customer is complaining about the delay.

Mary: Can you repeat the product serial number, sir?

Max: Yes, 00027405X2. Got that?

Mary: Let me repeat 00027405X2.

Max: That's correct. Now the deadline for the completion of the project has been brought forward to March 13, 2010, so he needs to get back to me by 4:30 today.

Mary: March 30, 2010 …

Max: No, that's March 13, 2010.

Mary: March 13, 2010, sorry, by 4.30 … OK.

Max: Also …

Mary: Hang on sir, I need more paper … OK.

Max: Also, can you ask him to confirm the amount of the last bill? I have $123,759, but I think it should be $275,264.

Mary: $123,759 or $275,264. OK, sir, I think I've got all those details. … Oh wait a moment, here is John! You can speak to him yourself now.

【中譯】

Max: 嗨，可以麻煩請 John 聽電話嗎？

Mary: 噢，對不起， John 現在在開會。

Max: 哦，他什麼時候有空？我有急事要跟他談。

Mary: 嗯……不確定。你要留言嗎？

Max: 好，你可以跟他說 Max 打電話來嗎？

Mary: Max ，好。他有你的電話號碼嗎？

Max: 沒有。我可以給你我的手機嗎？

Mary: 當然，請說。

Max: 號碼是 0953-125-487 。

Mary: 0953-125-487 。

Max: 沒錯。還有我的電話是 2274-7642 ，分機 274 。

Mary: 對不起，你可以再說一次嗎？

Max: 2274-7642 ，分機 274 。記下來了嗎？

Mary: 好了。

Max: 好，麻煩告訴他我們工廠產品編號 00027405X2 的規格有問題，必須等他跟我們釐清規格之後才能繼續。這個專案已經進度落後，而顧客也在抱怨了。

Mary: 你可以再說一次產品編號嗎？先生。

Max: 可以，00027405X2。記下來了嗎？

Mary: 我再重複一遍 00027405X2。

Max: 沒錯。現在這個案子的完成期限提前到 2010 年 3 月 13 日，所以他今天 4:30 以前必須回電給我。

Mary: 2010 年 3 月 30 日

Max: 不對，是 2010 年 3 月 13 日。

Mary: 2010 年 3 月 13 日，對不起，4:30 以前，好的。

Max: 還有……

Mary: 等一下，先生。我需要再拿張紙……好了。

Max: 還有，可不可以請他確認上一筆帳單的金額？我拿到的是 $123,759，不過我想應該是 $275,264 才對。

Mary: $123,759 或 $275,264。好的，先生。我想我已經把所有細節都記下來了……噢，等一下，John 來了。現在你可以自己跟他談了。

Track 068

Mr. Smith: Hello, Joan.

Joan: Hello, Mr. Smith. How was your meeting?

Mr. Smith: Yes, good, thanks. Are there any messages for me?

Joan: Oh yes, a few. Susan called from AIG.

Mr. Smith: Oh yes?

Joan: She didn't want to leave a message. But she asked you to call her back. Says it's urgent. She gave me the number of the office where she is going to be this afternoon, so you can call her there.

Mr. Smith: OK, what's the number?

Joan: It's 02-2678-6543, extension 678.

Mr. Smith: OK, extension 678. Got it.

Joan: She also gave me her cell phone number in case you can't reach her on the landline: it's 0953-285-684.

Mr. Smith: 0953-285-684.

Joan: That's right.

Mr. Smith: Anything else?

Joan: Yes, Mike called.

Mr. Smith: Oh. What did he want?

Joan: He says the amount on the last bill is way too high. Says it should be ... hang on, I've got the figures here ... says it should be $234,678, not $2,346,788.

Mr. Smith: Mm. Yes, that does sound a bit high. Oh. Probably a computer error with the last number. OK, I'll call him back. Anything else?

Joan: I booked your train to Kaohsiung. Leaves tomorrow morning at five past seven.

Mr. Smith: OK. Thanks for doing that.

Joan: And a customer called Wong Key called to ask about one of our products. I said you would need to speak to him 'cause I didn't know the product specs.

Mr. Smith: OK, what's the product number? Did you get it down?

Joan: Yes, I did. The number is XYW550007.

Mr. Smith: OK, I know.

Joan:	And then Mary called to remind you that the project deadline has been brought forward to the fourth of April 2009.
Mr. Smith:	Yes, I know. OK, thanks Joan.
Joan:	Can I have a break now?

【中譯】

Mr. Smith:	哈囉，Joan。
Joan:	哈囉，Smith 先生。會議進行得如何？
Mr. Smith:	很好，謝謝。有我的留言嗎？
Joan:	哦，有，有幾個。AIG 的 Susan 打電話來。
Mr. Smith:	哦，是嗎？
Joan:	她不想留言。不過她請你回電給她，說很緊急。她留了她下午會去的辦公室的電話號碼，你可以打去那裡找她。
Mr. Smith:	好，電話號碼多少？
Joan:	號碼是 02-2678-6543，分機 678。
Mr. Smith:	好，分機 678。記下了。
Joan:	她也給我她的手機號碼，以防萬一你打電話找不到她：號碼是 0953-285-684。
Mr. Smith:	0953-285-684。
Joan:	沒錯。
Mr. Smith:	還有嗎？
Joan:	有，Mike 打電話來。
Mr. Smith:	唔，他要做什麼？
Joan:	他說上一筆帳單的金額高出太多，說應該是……等一下，我把數字記在這裡……說應該是 $234,678，不是 $2,346,788。
Mr. Smith:	嗯……對，那的確聽起來有點高。唔，可能是電腦搞錯最後一個數字了。好吧，我會回電給他。還有其他事嗎？

Joan: 我幫你訂了到高雄的火車票，明天早上七點五分開車。

Mr. Smith: 好，謝謝妳幫忙。

Joan: 還有一位叫 Wong Key 的客戶打電話來問我們的一項產品。我說必須由你跟他談，因為我不知道產品的規格。

Mr. Smith: 好，產品編號多少？妳有記下來嗎？

Joan: 有，我記下來了。編號是 XYW550007。

Mr. Smith: 好，我知道了。

Joan: 還有 Mary 打電話來提醒你，專案的期限已經提前到 2009 年 4 月 4 日了。

Mr. Smith: 好，我知道了。嗯，謝啦，Joan。

Joan: 我現在可以休息了嗎？

Unit 11

That's Kris with a "K."

是有 K 的 Kris 。

學習重點 單字，你拼對了嗎？

聽聽看 **1** Kris 和 Mary 正在討論一些重要文件，你能聽懂多少呢？請再聽一遍，並完成下列表格。 Track 069

Courier Request Form

Recipient's name: ______________________

Recipient's address: ______________________

____

____

Contact number: 234-567-890

答案 請見 187 頁。

對很多人來說，在電話上留言或記下留言最困難的部分就是拼英文字母，無論是要聽、還是說給別人記下來。這個單元就是要加強各位這一部分的能力。

利用字母發音來聯想字母，對拼字會有幫助。接著我們來練習看看。

聽聽看 **2** 請聽 CD 播放的字母，並依據字母的發音將它們分類填入下表。（提示：字母中包含表頭單字底線部分的發音者，歸為同一類） Track 070

t<u>ea</u>	wh<u>e</u>n	tod<u>ay</u>	y<u>ou</u>	m<u>i</u>ne	f<u>ar</u>m	ph<u>o</u>ne
b						

答案 請見 187 頁。注意，在美式英語中 z 的發音是 /zi/，但在英式英語的發音卻是 /zed/。此外，在英式英語中 r 的發音是 /ɑ/，不捲舌的。

接著來挑戰更困難的：多個字母合併一起使用的情況。

動動腦

3 請看下列縮寫。它們是以字母發音所做的歸類，請找出每一組中與其他縮寫發音不相同者，把它圈起來。如範例。接著請聽 CD 中的唸法，看看你是否想修改答案。

Track 071

1	COD	BOT	FOB	POD
2	MIT	NEC	NYC	FIT
3	VAT	CAP	BKG	PLC
4	GDP	PST	GMT	GNP
5	EGM	CIF	DCF	PPS

答案 請見 187 頁。核對完答案，請跟著 CD 練習這些縮寫的唸法。

聽聽看

4 請再聽一次 CD，如果不看上一題的文字，你有把握能把聽到的縮寫都正確地寫下來嗎。 Track 071

1. ______________________________

2. ______________________________

3. ______________________________

4. ______________________________

5. ______________________________

最容易搞錯的字母是 w，當它和其他「雙重字母」一起出現時，發音非常相近：例如： uu（唸成 double u）、ll（唸成 double l）。

說說看

5 請看下列這些常見的英文名字。試著練習拼出這些名字。

1. Williams
2. Widdowson
3. Wood
4. Waddle
5. Weed
6. Willow
7. Walker
8. Wilder
9. Woodrow
10. Willson

聽聽看

6 請聽 CD 並寫下你所聽到的名字。

Track 072

1. ____________
2. ____________
3. ____________
4. ____________
5. ____________
6. ____________
7. ____________
8. ____________
9. ____________
10. ____________

答案 發現了嗎，答案其實就是上一題的人名，只是調換了順序。請跟著 CD 覆誦，多練習幾次人名的拼法。

在聽寫名字或住址時，爲了避免錯誤，你可能需要再次確認你所記下的內容。接著就來學習一些相關的用語。

動動腦 7 請將下列用語分類填入表格中。

- Can you read that back to me?
- Can you spell that for me, please?
- Could you spell that, please?
- Have you got that?
- How do you spell that, please?
- Is that double X or one X?
- Is that right?
- Let me spell it for you.
- That's Y with an X.
- Would you like me to spell it for you?

留言者	記下留言者

答案 請見 188 頁。

說說看 8 請跟著 CD 覆誦，練習這些字串的發音。

Track 073

想要更熟悉這些字串的用法，可以回頭聽聽 Track 069，並留意它們在上下文中如何使用。

聽聽看

9 現在請聽另一段電話對談。聽的時候，請一邊完成下列表格。專注在本單元所學的重點，看看你進步了多少。

Track 074

New Customer Enquiry Form

Name:	______________________
Address:	39 ______________________
	__________ Industrial Estate
	__________ England
Enquiry:	new catalogue

答案 請見 188 頁。

解答

聽聽看 1

Courier Request Form

Recipient's name:	**Mr. Kris Walker**
Recipient's address:	**Widdowson House, Villiers Street,**
	Number 43, 4th floor
Contact number:	234-567-890

聽聽看 2

tea	when	today	you	mine	farm	phone
b g	f n	a	q	i	r	o
c p	l s	h	u	y		
d t	m x	j	w			
e v		k				

動動腦 3

1	COD	BOT	**FOB**	POD
2	MIT	**NEC**	NYC	FIT
3	VAT	CAP	BKG	**PLC**
4	**GDP**	PST	GMT	GNP
5	EGM	**CIF**	DCF	PPS

動動腦 7

留言者	記下留言者
• **That's Y with an X.** 那是有 X 的 Y。 • **Would you like me to spell it for you?** 你要我幫你拼出來嗎？ • **Let me spell it for you.** 我幫你拼出來。 • **Have you got that?** 你記下來了嗎？ • **Can you read that back to me?** 你可以唸給我聽看看嗎？	• **Could you spell that, please?** 可以請你拼一下嗎？ • **How do you spell that, please?** 請問那個字怎麼拼？ • **Can you spell that for me, please?** 你可以幫我拼一下嗎？ • **Is that right?** 這樣對嗎？ • **Is that double X or one X?** 是二個 X 還是一個 X？

聽聽看 9

New Customer Enquiry Form

Name: **Winston Owen (Mr.)**

Address: 39 **Willow Road**

Stowerbridge Industrial Estate

Stow England

Enquiry: new catalogue

CD 內容

Track 069

（Kris ：英國口音）

Kris: Hi Mary, did you send the documents yet?

Mary: Not yet, they're sitting in front of me. Is it urgent?

Kris: Yes, of course. I need them right away!

Mary: Oh, sorry, I didn't realize. I'll take them to the post office now.

Kris: No, that will take too long. I need them by this afternoon. Can you send them by courier?

Mary: Sure. Mm ... you will need to give me the address.

Kris: OK. You got a pen?

Mary: Hang on. OK. Now, the name is Chris Walker, isn't it?

Kris: That's right, and that's Kris with a K.

Mary: OK, and Walker is W-A-L-K-E-R, right?

Kris: Right. The address is: Widdowson House, Villiers Street, number 43, 4th floor.

Mary: How do you spell that, please?

Kris: V-I-L-L-I-E-R-S

Mary: And Widdowson?

Kris: W-I-D-D-O-W-S-O-N

Mary: OK, got it. Number 43, 4th floor. OK, Kris, I'll get them off to you right away.

Kris: Thanks.

【中譯】

Kris: 嗨，Mary，妳把文件寄出來了沒有？

Mary: 還沒有，還擺在我前面。很緊急嗎？

Kris: 對，當然囉。我馬上就要！

Mary: 唔，對不起，我不知道。我現在就拿去郵局寄。

Kris: 不，那樣太慢了。我今天下午就要，妳可以用快遞寄給我嗎？

Mary: 沒問題。嗯……你得給我住址。

Kris: 好，妳有筆嗎？

Mary: 等一下。好了。所以，名字是 Chris Walker ，對吧？

Kris: 沒錯，是有一個 K 的 Kris 。

Mary: 好，然後 Walker 是 W-A-L-K-E-R ，對吧？

Kris: 對。住址是： Widdowson 大樓 Villiers 街 43 號 4 樓。

Mary: 請問那要怎麼拼？

Kris: V-I-L-L-I-E-R-S 。

Mary: 還有 Widdowson 呢？

Kris: W-I-D-D-O-W-S-O-N 。

Mary: 好，記下來了。43 號 4 樓。好， Kris ，我馬上就把文件寄給你。

Kris: 謝謝。

Track 070

A-B-C-D-E-F-G-H-I-J-K-L-M-N-O-P-Q-R-S-T-U-V-W-X-Y-Z

Track 072

1. W-A-D-D-L-E
2. W-A-L-K-E-R
3. W-E-E-D
4. W-I-D-D-O-W-S-O-N
5. W-I-L-D-E-R
6. W-I-L-L-I-A-M-S
7. W-I-L-L-O-W
8. W-I-L-L-S-O-N
9. W-O-O-D
10. W-O-O-D-R-O-W

Track 074

（Man：英國口音）

Mary: Hello, Cheaper Plastics Ltd.

Man: Hello, I wonder if you could send me your latest catalog please.

Mary: Yes, of course. Are you already a customer, sir?

Man: No, not yet.

Mary: OK. Just hold on a minute, please sir, and I'll take down your details.

Man: Thanks.

Mary: OK. What's your name, sir?

Man: Winston Owen.

Mary: Can you spell that for me, please?

Man: Yes, that's W-I-N-S-T-O-N new word O-W-E-N. Can you read that back to me?

Mary: W-I-N-S-T-O-N O-W-E-N.

Man: That's correct. And my address is 39 Willow Road, Stowerbridge Industrial Estate, Stow, England.

Mary: Just a moment. Willow Road, is that double l or one l?

Man: Double l, W-I-L-L-O-W.

Mary: Could you spell Stowerbridge for me, sir?

Man: S-T-O-W-E-R-B-R-I-D-G-E.

Mary: S-T-O-W-E-R-B-R-I-D-G-E.

Man: Can you read that back to me?

Mary: 39 Willow Road, Stowerbridge Industrial Estate, Stow, S-T-O-W, England.

Man: That's correct.

Mary: I'll put a catalogue in the post for you right away, sir.

Man: Thank you!

【中譯】

Mary: 嗨，Cheaper Plastics 公司。

Man: 哈囉，我在想是不是可以請你們寄最新的目錄給我？

Mary: 是，當然可以。你已經是我們的顧客嗎，先生？

Man: 不，還不是。

Mary: 好的，請稍待一下，先生，我把你的詳細資料記下來。

Man: 謝謝。

Mary: 好，請問大名，先生？

Man: Winston Owen。

Mary: 可以請你幫我拼出來嗎？

Man: 好，就是 W-I-N-S-T-O-N，新字 O-W-E-N。妳可以唸一次給我聽嗎？

Mary: W-I-N-S-T-O-N O-W-E-N。

Man: 沒錯。還有我的住址是英格蘭 Stow 市，Stowerbridge 工業區 Willow 路 39 號。

Mary: 等一下。Willow 路，那是兩個 l，還是一個 l？

Man: 兩個 l，W-I-L-L-O-W。

Mary: 你可以幫我把 Stowerbridge 拼出來嗎，先生？

Man: S-T-O-W-E-R-B-R-I-D-G-E。

Mary: S-T-O-W-E-R-B-R-I-D-G-E。

Man: 妳可以唸一次給我聽嗎？

Mary: 英格蘭 Stow 市，S-T-O-W，Stowerbridge 工業區 Willow 路 39 號。

Man: 沒錯。

Mary: 我馬上就幫你郵寄一份目錄，先生。

Man: 謝謝妳！

Unit 12

Sorry, That's Taiwan, Not Thailand.

不好意思，是台灣，不是泰國。

學習重點 是對還是錯，注意聽語調！

聽聽看

1 **Mary 正在接一位顧客的詢問電話，請問來電者想知道哪些事情？請一邊聽一邊完成下列表格。** Track 075

New Customer Enquiry Form

Name:	Mr.
Contact:	Burlington, Virginia
	Tel:
Enquiry:	product number: other colors?

答案 請見 201 頁。

本單元整合了前兩個單元的學習重點，並針對電話留言做進一步的練習。記留言時，有時候會發生誤解訊息的狀況。在此情況下，留言者會糾正訊息。能夠聽出何者爲正確訊息、何者又爲誤，是很重要的。而判斷的關鍵就在「語調」。在這個單元，我們要學習的就是更正訊息的語調。

說說看

2 **下列為糾正訊息的字串，請跟著 CD 覆誦，練習它們的唸法。** Track 076

- **No, X, not Y.** 不，是 X，不是 Y。
- **That should be X, not Y.** 應該是 X，不是 Y。
- **That's X, not Y.** 那是 X，不是 Y。
- **Sorry, I mean X, not Y.** 不好意思，我是指 X，不是 Y。

分析

- 注意，在每一個字串中，都先告知正確訊息。
- 雖然正確訊息先出現，但判斷正確訊息的關鍵是語調，並不是出現的先後順序。
- 在每一個字串中，正確訊息的語調會提高，而錯誤訊息的語調會降低，如下所示：

No, X not Y.

That should be X, not Y.

That's X, not Y.

Sorry, I mean X, not Y.

請照著語調重點的教學，再多練習幾次上述字串的唸法，讓自己可以自然地以相同語調模式說出這些字串。接著我們來練習聽力，看看你是否能藉由語調來聽出正確訊息。

聽聽看

3 請聽 CD 並將下列正確訊息打勾。請見範例。

Track 077

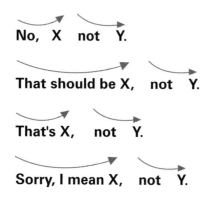

1	✔	40		14
2		1457		1456
3		Thursday		Tuesday
4		2009		2008

5		Willow		Widdow
6		John		Don
7		Dean Street		Dean Road
8		M-A-R-I-E		M-A-R-Y
9		current number		previous number
10		2P		2B
11		today		tomorrow
12		France		French
13		this week		next week
14		green		blue
15		2000		200

答案 請見201頁。

有時候，正確訊息會出現在句子的最後。在這種情況下，語調的規則還是一樣：正確訊息的語調抬高；錯誤訊息的語調則降低。

說說看

4 下列為糾正訊息的字串，請跟著CD覆誦，練習它們的唸法。 Track 078

- **No, not Y, X.** 不，不是Y，是X。
- **Not Y, that should be X.** 不是Y，那應該是X。
- **Not Y, that's X.** 不是Y，是X。
- **Sorry, I don't mean Y, I mean X.** 不好意思，我不是指Y，是X。

分析

▸▸ 每一個字串的正確訊息都出現在句尾。

- 雖然正確訊息最後出現，但判斷正確訊息關鍵的是語調，不是訊息出現的先後順序。
- 在每一個字串中，正確訊息的語調會抬高，錯誤訊息的語調則會降低，如下所示：

No, not Y,　X.

Not Y,　that should be X.

Not Y,　that's X.

Sorry, I don't mean Y,　I mean X.

請照著語調重點的教學，再多練習幾次上述字串的唸法，讓自己可以自然地以相同語調模式說出這些字串。接著我們來練習聽力，看看你是否能藉由語調來聽出正確訊息。

聽聽看

5 請聽 CD 並將下列正確訊息打勾。請見範例。

Track 079

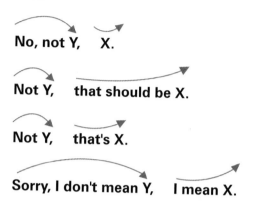

1		Sunday	✔	Monday
2		30		13
3		Taiwan		Thailand
4		Widder		Witter
5		this week		last week
6		500		50,000
7		Holland		Germany

8		blue		red
9		3T		3D
10		the 25th		the 26th
11		tomorrow		the day after tomorrow
12		2791		2790
13		UK		US
14		Peter		Dieter
15		P-Y-E		P-I-E

答案 請見202頁。

到目前爲止，我們已經學了兩種字串：正確訊息先出現的字串，如：That should be X, not Y.，以及正確訊息最後出現的字串，如：Not Y, that should be X.。記得，無論是哪一種字串，判斷正確訊息的關鍵是語調。現在我們來綜合練習此二種字串。

動動腦 **6** 請將下列字串分類填入下頁的表格。 Track 080

- No, X, not Y.
- Not Y, that should be X.
- That should be X, not Y.
- No, not Y, X.
- Sorry, I mean X, not Y.
- Not Y, that's X.
- Sorry, I don't mean Y. I mean X.
- That's X, not Y.

正確訊息先出現	正確訊息後出現

答案 請見 202 頁。核對完答案，請練習跟著 Track 080 覆誦，留意自己的語調。

聽聽看 **7 現在請聽 CD 並勾選正確訊息。** Track 081

1	✔	T40		D14
2		w		double l
3		1256		1265
4		Monday		Tuesday
5		Julia		Julie
6		A15		A50
7		DODD		DODT
8		PNG		BNG
9		next Friday		tomorrow
10		October		August
11		Campus Road		Campus Street
12		OURX		UORX
13		25,000 units		250,000 units
14		airmail		surface mail

15		board meeting		AGM
16		Vienna		Vietnam

答案 請見203頁。記住，聽的重點在於語調，不是文法。如果你沒辦法完全答對，請多練習幾次。

聽聽看

8 現在請聽另一段電話對談，聽的時候請一邊完成下列表格。請專注在本單元所學到的重點，看看你進步了多少。

Track 082

Courier Request Form

Recipient's name: Mr. ________ Sung ________

Recipient's address: ________ Dunhua North Road

________ Floor ________

____

Contact number: ________________

答案 請見203頁。

解答

聽聽看 1

New Customer Enquiry Form

Name: Mr. **Ted Willson**

Contact: Burlington, Virginia

Tel: **1-304-558-2960**

Enquiry: product number: **2769XT** other colors?

聽聽看 3

1	✔	40		14
2		1457	✔	1456
3		Thursday	✔	Tuesday
4	✔	2009		2008
5		Willow	✔	Widdow
6	✔	John		Don
7	✔	Dean Street		Dean Road
8		M-A-R-I-E	✔	M-A-R-Y
9	✔	current number		previous number
10		2P	✔	2B
11	✔	today		tomorrow
12	✔	France		French
13		this week	✔	next week
14		green	✔	blue
15		2000	✔	200

聽聽看 5

1		Sunday	✔	Monday
2		30	✔	13
3	✔	Taiwan		Thailand
4	✔	Widder		Witter
5	✔	this week		last week
6		500	✔	50,000
7		Holland	✔	Germany
8	✔	blue		red
9		3T	✔	3D
10		the 25th	✔	the 26th
11		tomorrow	✔	the day after tomorrow
12	✔	2791		2790
13	✔	UK		US
14		Peter	✔	Dieter
15	✔	P-Y-E		P-I-E

動動腦 6

正確訊息先出現	正確訊息後出現
• **No, X, not Y.** • **That should be X, not Y.** • **Sorry, I mean X, not Y.** • **That's X, not Y.**	• **Not Y, that should be X.** • **No, not Y, X.** • **Not Y, that's X.** • **Sorry, I don't mean Y. I mean X.**

聽聽看 7

1	✔	T40		D14
2		w	✔	double l
3		1256	✔	1265
4		Monday	✔	Tuesday
5		Julia	✔	Julie
6	✔	A15		A50
7	✔	DODD		DODT
8		PNG	✔	BNG
9	✔	next Friday		tomorrow
10	✔	October		August
11		Campus Road	✔	Campus Street
12	✔	OURX		UORX
13	✔	25,000 units		250,000 units
14		airmail	✔	surface mail
15	✔	board meeting		AGM
16		Vienna	✔	Vietnam

聽聽看 8

Courier Request Form

Recipient's name: Mr. **Stephen** Sung

Recipient's address: **240/15** Dunhua North Road

8th Floor

Contact number: **0953 124 988**

CD 內容

Track 075

Mary: Formosa Bathroom Rubber, how can I help you?

Ted: Yes, hello, I'm calling from Burlington, Virginia in America. I'd like to ask you a few questions about a few of your products.

Mary: Sure. Which products would you like to ask about?

Ted: Mmm. I'm looking at your catalogue here, and I'd like to ask about product number 2769XT.

Mary: OK, hang on, let me get the catalogue. OK. What page is that?

Ted: Page 17.

Mary: Page 70, OK ...

Ted: No, 17, not 70.

Mary: Oh, sorry. OK. Product number 2796XT?

Ted: Not 2796XT, that should be 2769XT.

Mary: Oh, sorry, OK. The plastic ducks?

Ted: Yes. In the picture they're yellow, but I would like to know what other colors you have.

Mary: Um, I'm going to have to get someone to call you back about that. Can you give me your number?

Ted: Sure. You got a pen?

Mary: Yes, go ahead.

Ted: OK, my name is Mr. Ted Willson. W-I-L-L-S-O-N.

Mary: W-I-L-S-O-N.

Ted: That's double 1, not one l.

Mary: W-I-L-L-S-O-N.

Ted: Correct. And my number is 1-304-558-2960.

Mary: 1-30-558-2960

Ted: Not 1-30-558-2960, that's 304-558.

Mary: OK, let me read that back to you: 1-304-558-2960.

Ted: That's correct.

Mary: I'll get someone to call you back right away, Mr. Willson.

Ted: Thanks.

【中譯】

Mary: Formosa Bathroom Rubber 公司，有什麼我能為您效勞嗎？

Ted: 是，哈囉，我這裡是美國維吉尼亞州的 Burlington 公司。我想請問妳一些關於貴公司幾項產品的問題。

Mary: 當然。你想問的是關於哪些產品呢？

Ted: 嗯……我在這邊正看著你們的目錄，我想詢問關於產品編號 2769XT 的問題。

Mary: 好，請稍候，我拿一下目錄。好了。那是在哪一頁？

Ted: 第 17 頁。

Mary: 第 70 頁，好……

Ted: 不對，是 17 ，不是 70 。

Mary: 哦，對不起。好。產品序號 2796XT ？

Ted: 不是 2796XT ，應該是 2769XT 。

Mary: 哦，對不起。好。塑膠鴨子？

Ted: 是的。圖片上的鴨子是黃色的，可是我想知道你們有哪些其他顏色？

Mary: 唔……關於這個我必須找別人回電給你。你可以給我你的電話嗎？

Ted: 當然，你有筆嗎？

Mary: 有，請說。

Ted: 好，我的名字是 Ted Willson ， W-I-L-L-S-O-N 。

Mary: W-I-L-S-O-N。

Ted: 是兩個 L，不是一個 L。

Mary: W-I-L-L-S-O-N。

Ted: 沒錯。還有我的電話是 1-304-558-2960。

Mary: 1-30-558-2960。

Ted: 不是 1-30-558-2960，是 304-558。

Mary: 好。讓我唸一次給你聽： 1-304-558-2960。

Ted: 沒錯。

Mary: 我會請人馬上回電給你，Willson 先生。

Ted: 謝謝。

Track 077

1. No, 40, not 14.
2. That should be 1456, not 1457.
3. That's Tuesday, not Thursday.
4. Sorry, I mean 2009, not 2008.
5. No, Widdow, not Willow.
6. That should be John, not Don.
7. Sorry, I mean Dean Street, not Dean Road.
8. No, MARY, not MARIE.
9. That should be the current number, not the previous one.
10. That's 2B, not 2P.
11. Sorry, I mean today, not tomorrow.
12. No, France, not French.
13. That should be next week, not this week.
14. That's blue, not green.
15. Sorry, I mean 200, not 2000.

【中譯】

1. 不，是 40 ，不是 14 。
2. 應該是 1456 ，不是 1457 。
3. 是星期二，不是星期四。
4. 不好意思，我指的是 2009 ，不是 2008 。
5. 不對，是 Widdow ，不是 Willow 。
6. 應該是 John ，不是 Don 。
7. 不好意思，我指的是 Dean 街，不是 Dean 路。
8. 不，是 MARY ，不是 MARIE 。
9. 那應該是目前的數字，不是先前的。
10. 是 2B ，不是 2P 。
11. 不好意思，我指的是今天，不是明天。
12. 不，是法國，不是法文。
13. 應該是下週，不是本週。
14. 是藍色，不是綠色。
15. 不好意思，我指的是 200 ，不是 2000 。

Track 079

1. Not Sunday, that's Monday.
2. No, not 30, 13.
3. Not Thailand, that should be Taiwan.
4. Not Witter, that's Widder.
5. Sorry, I don't mean last week, I mean this week.
6. No, not 500, 50,000.
7. Not Holland, that should be Germany.
8. Not red, that's blue.
9. Sorry, I don't mean 3T. I mean 3D.

10. No, not the 25th, the 26th.

11. Not tomorrow, that should be the day after tomorrow.

12. Not 2790, that's 2791.

13. Sorry, I don't mean US. I mean UK.

14. Not Peter, that should be Dieter.

15. Not P-I-E, that's P-Y-E.

【中譯】

---

1. 不是週日，是週一。
2. 不，不是 30 ，是 13 。
3. 不是泰國，應該是台灣。
4. 不是 Witter ，是 Widder 。
5. 不好意思，我指的不是上週，我指的是本週。
6. 不，不是 500 ，是 50,000 。
7. 不是荷蘭，應該是德國。
8. 不是紅色，是藍色。
9. 不好意思，我指的不是 3T ，我指的是 3D 。
10. 不，不是 25 日，是 26 日。
11. 不是明天，應該是後天。
12. 不是 2790 ，是 2791 。
13. 不好意思，我指的不是美國，我指的是英國。
14. 不是 Peter ，應該是 Dieter 。
15. 不是 P-I-E ，是 P-Y-E 。

Track 081

1. Sorry, I mean T40, not D14.

2. Not w, that's double l.

3. That should be 1265, not 1256.

4. No, not Monday, Tuesday.

5. No, Julie, not Julia.

6. Not A50, that should be A15.

7. That's DODD, not DODT.

8. Not PNG, that should be BNG.

9. Sorry, I don't mean tomorrow. I mean next Friday.

10. No, not August, October.

11. Sorry, I mean Campus Street, not Campus Road.

12. No, OURX, not UORX.

13. That should be 25,000 units, not 250,000 units.

14. Sorry, I don't mean airmail. I mean surface mail.

15. That's for the board meeting, not the AGM.

16. Not Vienna, that's Vietnam.

【中譯】

1. 不好意思，我指的是 T40 ，不是 D14 。
2. 不是 w ，是二個 l 。
3. 應該是 1265 ，不是 1256 。
4. 不，不是週一，是週二。
5. 不，是 Julie ，不是 Julia 。
6. 不是 A50 ，應該是 A15 。
7. 是 DODD ，不是 DODT 。
8. 不是 PNG ，應該是 BNG 。
9. 不好意思，我指的不是明天，我指的是下週五。
10. 不，不是八月，是十月。
11. 不好意思，我指的是 Campus 街，不是 Campus 路。

12. 不，是 OURX，不是 UORX。

13. 應該是 25,000 件，不是 250,000 件。

14. 不好意思，我指的不是空運，我指的是海運。

15. 那是為了董事會議，不是 AGM。

16. 不是維也納，是越南。

Track 082

Mary: Hello Formosa Bathroom Rubber, how can I help you?

Stephen: Hello? Hello, hello?

Mary: Hello? Can you hear me?

Stephen: Yes, I can now. Er, hi, I'm still waiting for the catalogue you promised me.

Mary: Oh really? When did you order it?

Stephen: Last month, and it still hasn't arrived.

Mary: Oh, that's terrible. I'm sorry. Are you in Taiwan?

Stephen: Yes, in Taipei.

Mary: Oh, OK. Would you like to leave me your contact details, and I'll make sure a catalogue gets couriered round to your office this afternoon?

Stephen: What?

Mary: Would you like to leave me your contact details, and I'll make sure a catalogue gets couriered to your office this afternoon?

Stephen: Oh, that's very kind of you. Yes. My address is Dunhua North Road, number 240/14, eighth floor.

Mary: OK, hang on. Dunhua North Road number 240/14 …

Stephen: Sorry, I mean 240/15, not 14. We just moved across the hall and I keep forgetting to remember.

Mary: Oh, 240/15, ninth floor, did you say?

Stephen: No, not ninth, eighth.

Mary: Eighth floor. OK. And your name is?

Stephen: Stephen Sung.

Mary: S-T-E-V-E-N Sung.

Stephen: That should be P-H, not V. S-T-E-P-H-E-N.

Mary: Oh, I'm sorry Mr. Sung. Can you leave me your mobile number?

Stephen: Sure. 0953-124-998.

Mary: 0953-124-998.

Stephen: Sorry, I don't mean 998, I mean 988. Sorry, it's a new number and I have problems remembering it.

Mary: 0953-124-988?

Stephen: Yes, that's right.

Mary: Are you sure?

Stephen: Yes, pretty sure. Mmm wait. No. Yes! It's right. Ha ha. Sorry.

Mary: OK, Mr. Sung, I'll get the catalogue delivered to your office.

Stephen: Thanks.

【中譯】

Mary: 哈囉，Formosa Bathroom Rubber 公司，有什麼我能夠為您效勞嗎？

Stephen: 哈囉？哈囉，哈囉？

Mary: 哈囉？你聽得見我嗎？

Stephen: 是，我現在可以了。呃，嗨，我還在等你們答應要寄給我的目錄。

Mary: 哦，真的嗎？你是什麼時候訂的？

Stephen: 上個月，到現在還沒到。

Mary: 哦，真糟糕。我很抱歉。你人在台灣嗎？

Stephen: 對，在台北。

Mary: 哦，好。可以把你的詳細連絡方式留給我嗎？我會確保今天下午就把目錄快遞送到你的辦公室。

Stephen: 什麼？

Mary: 可以把你的連絡細節留給我嗎？我會確保今天下午就把目錄快遞送去你的辦公室。

Stephen: 喔，妳人真好。好的。我的住址是敦化北路 240 之 14 號 8 樓。

Mary: 好，等一下。敦化北路 240 之 14 號……

Stephen: 對不起，我指的是 240 之 15 號，不是 14 。我們剛搬到對門，而我老是忘記。

Mary: 喔， 240 之 15 ， 9 樓，是這樣嗎？

Stephen: 不，不是 9 樓，是 8 樓。

Mary: 8 樓。好，那你的名字是？

Stephen: Stephen 宋。

Mary: S-T-E-V-E-N 宋。

Stephen: 應該是 P-H ，不是 V 。 S-T-E-P-H-E-N 。

Mary: 喔，對不起，宋先生。你可以把手機號碼留給我嗎？

Stephen: 當然。 0953-124-998 。

Mary: 0953-124-998 。

Stephen: 對不起，我指的不是 998 ，我指的是 988 。不好意思，這是新號碼，我一直記不起來。

Mary: 0953-124-988 ？

Stephen: 是，沒錯。

Mary: 你確定？

Stephen: 是，相當確定。嗯……等一下。不。對！沒錯。哈哈。對不起。

Mary: 好的，宋先生。我會把目錄寄到你的辦公室。

Stephen: 謝謝。

Part 4

簡報篇

Presentation

Unit 13

Don't Sweat the Small Stuff.

別為小事傷神啊。

學習重點 聽到閃神沒關係，抓住關鍵字就好！

聽聽看

1 **Joanna 針對目前市場情況做了一段簡報，你可以聽懂多少呢？請判斷下列訊息為 True 還是 False 。**

Track 083

		True	False
1	Joanna 談論的是當地市場情況。		
2	失業率持穩。		
3	人們在商店裡的消費增加。		
4	銀行通過的貸款申請減少。		
5	房屋和公寓強制回收增加。		
6	出口量增加。		
7	借貸保險愈來愈難取得。		
8	當地匯率已經受到影響。		

答案 請見 224 頁。

聽英文簡報不是件簡單的事，因爲有很多訊息要吸收，中間還隔著一層語言的障礙。你可能擔心自己沒辦法聽清楚每個字而遺漏重要訊息，於是簡報全程繃緊神經，試圖想要掌握簡報者的每一字句，其實不須如此費力。並不是簡報者所說的每一個字都是重要的。你必須掌握的是重要關鍵字，不必擔心瑣碎字句。換句話說就是： Don't sweat the small stuff！在這個單元中，就是要培養各位聽關鍵字的能力。

首先，必須了解「意義字」和「功能字」之間的差異。意義字就是用來表達想法的內容字；功能字則是沒有意義、但具有文法功能的字。

動動腦

2 **請將下列字彙歸類，填入表格。**

■ and	■ enormous	■ has	■ in
■ inform	■ price	■ reduce	■ small
■ strategy	■ the	■ a	■ you

意義字	功能字

答案 請見 224 頁。核對完答案，請閱讀下列說明事項。

分 析

- 意義字可能是名詞、動詞或形容詞。不過，不用太擔心此種文法上的詞性分類，只要記得它們是句子裡具有意義的字，也就是訊息。當你在聽人說話時，它們是重要的。

- 功能字通常是代名詞、介系詞、連接詞或助動詞。同樣地，不用擔心這些詞性分類，只要記得它們在傳達訊息上扮演的不是重要角色。當你在聽人說話時，它們通常不是重要字詞。

- Have 可以當意義字（作動詞），例：I have a new car.，也可當功能字（作助動詞），例：She has completed the report.。

- 在口語上，要判別 have 是哪種用途很簡單。have 當成意義字使用時，會重讀，你可以清楚聽見它；如果是當成功能字使用，通常會輕讀，你很難清楚聽見它。

一般來說，意義字會重讀，而功能字不會。

動動腦 **3 請看下列句子，並將意義字畫上底線。**

1. First, I'm going to talk about the background. Then, I'm going to make some proposals for dealing with the problem.
2. I'd like to look in a bit more detail at the results of the survey for each segment of the market.
3. All the respondents said they would like to own more of the product line.
4. The situation has been getting worse for a while, and if we don't take action, it will damage the company.
5. Sales rose by 20% in this period last year, but this year they have only risen by 5%. This is a very bad situation.
6. If you look here, you can see that this supplier's prices are the highest.
7. These figures suggest that the strategy has worked so far.

答案 請見224頁。

核對完答案之後，我來進一步說明：

1. **First, I'm going to talk about the background. Then, I'm going to make some proposals for dealing with the problem.**

說明 普通名詞和動詞會重讀。不過像first和then這些字也會，它們屬於架構字 (organizing words)，幫助你聽懂簡報的起承轉合。助動詞以及像the和to這些微不足道的字則都不會重讀。

2. I'd like to look in a bit more detail at the results of the survey for each segment of the market.

說明 名詞、動詞，還有each都會重讀，each有強調語意的作用。

3. All the respondents said they would like to own more of the product line.

說明 all和more這些字會重讀，因爲它們都有說明語意的功能。例如：All respondents, not just some of them.。

4. The situation has been getting worse for a while, and if we don't take action, it will damage the company.

說明 否定助動詞會重讀，如：don't、can't、haven't、isn't。

5. Sales rose by 20% in this period last year, but this year they have only risen by 5%. This is a very bad situation.

說明 動作、數據都會重讀。其他像this和that這些字也會重讀，因爲它們通常會指出何者是重要的，如：this one、this year。

6. If you look here, you can see that this supplier's prices are the highest.

說明 除了名詞和動詞，here也會重讀，因爲簡報者希望把焦點聚集在投影片的某個地方。

7. These figures suggest that the strategy has worked so far.

說明 普通名詞和動詞會重讀。

所以嚕，聽簡報時不用試圖了解每一個字，專注於重讀的字就好。一般來說，這樣子就足以聽懂句子的意思了。

聽聽看

4 現在請聽上一題的句子，留意句中的字是如何重讀與輕讀。 Track 084

你對於句子的輕重音如何表現應該比較有概念了，接著，來加強各位聽關鍵字的聽力習慣。

聽聽看

5 請聽 CD 播放的句子。聽的時候請搭配下列的句中關鍵字。 Track 085

1. First talk overseas markets. Then discuss problems home market.
2. Each store chain did well last year, sales all stores doing very well.
3. Don't have distributors market really able increase market share.
4. Costs rose 33% last quarter increase price oil. Not acceptable.
5. Here figures last quarter, last year.

答案 查覺到了嗎？上列的關鍵字即為句中需要重讀的字，也就是意義字。你能否藉由聽出這些關鍵字，理解句子所要表達的意思呢？完整句子可參閱本章末的 CD 內容。

聽聽看

6 接著聽聽另外 5 個句子，這次請將輕讀字填入空格內，每個空格可能不只一個字。 Track 086

1. ________ have ________ lay off ________ least one-third ________ workforce ________ this recession continues.

2. ________ can't increase ________ sales ________ current number ________ sales staff.

3. ________ didn't enter this market ________ one year ________, ________ that's ________ things ________ slow here.

4. ________ volume ________ trade ________ slowed down ________ difficulties ________ obtaining credit.

5. Bad weather ________ delayed ________ shipments this month.

答案 請見 225 頁。

聽聽看

7 請聽句子，並從下列字彙挑選正確者填入空格內。 Track 087

■ 6%	■ increased	■ prices	■ situation
■ bad	■ market	■ risen	■ up
■ costs	■ oil	■ share	■ very
■ declined	■ price	■ sharply	

1. ________ have ________ ________.

2. We ________ our ________.

3. The ________ is ________ ________.

4. ________ ________ has ________.

5. The ________ of ________ went ________ ________.

答案 請見225頁。

聽聽看 8 請再聽另外 5 個句子，並填空。 Track 088

1. I would like to ________ the ________ ________.

2. We should ________ our ________ by ________.

3. This ________ is ________ ________ ________.

4. The ________ are ________ ________ for ________.

5. ________ ________ is ________, but the ________ ________ ________ is ________.

答案 請見225頁。

上面接連幾個練習，都是要強化各位聽關鍵字的習慣。記住，不要試圖聽懂每一個字，掌握句中的意義字即可，而意義字通常會重讀。

聽聽看

9 現在請聽另一段簡報。George 在一家製造與銷售機械產品的公司上班。聽的時候，請判斷下列陳述為 True 還是 False 。請專注在本單元所學到的重點，看看你進步了多少。 Track 089

		True	False
1	George 在談論關於採購部門的事。		
2	業績狀況良好。		
3	業績在過去這一季提高了 3% 。		
4	消費者的支出凍結。		
5	業務團隊工作很賣力。		
6	業務團隊專注從既有客戶取得更大筆的訂單。		
7	新客戶在詢問折扣。		
8	這一季的利潤會減少。		

答案 請見 226 頁。

解答

聽聽看 1

		True	False
1	Joanna 談論的是當地市場情況。	✔	
2	失業率持穩。		✔
3	人們在商店裡的消費增加。		✔
4	銀行通過的貸款申請減少。	✔	
5	房屋和公寓強制回收增加。	✔	
6	出口量增加。		✔
7	借貸保險愈來愈難取得。	✔	
8	當地匯率已經受到影響。	✔	

動動腦 2

意義字		功能字	
reduce	price	you	and
inform	enormous	the	a
strategy	small	in	has

動動腦 3

1. **First**, I'm going to **talk** about the **background**. **Then**, I'm going to **make** some **proposals** for **dealing** with the **problem**.
2. I'd like to **look** in a bit more **detail** at the **results** of the **survey** for **each segment** of the **market**.
3. **All** the **respondents** said they would like to **own more** of the **product line**.

4. The **situation** has been **getting worse** for a while, and if we **don't take action**, it will **damage** the **company**.
5. **Sales rose** by **20%** in **this period last** year, but **this** year they have **only risen** by **5%**. **This** is a **very bad situation**.
6. If you look **here**, you can **see** that this **supplier's prices** are the **highest**.
7. These **figures suggest** that the **strategy** has **worked** so **far**.

聽聽看 6

1. **We are going to** have **to** lay off **at** least one-third **of our** workforce **if** this recession continues.
2. **We** can't increase **our** sales **with the** current number **of** sales staff.
3. **We** didn't enter this market **until** one year **ago**, **so** that's **why** things **are** slow here.
4. **The** volume **of** trade **has** slowed down **due to** difficulties **in** obtaining credit.
5. Bad weather **has again** delayed **the** shipments this month.

聽聽看 7

1. **Costs** have **risen sharply**.
2. We **increased** our **prices**.
3. The **situation** is **very bad**.
4. **Market share** has **declined**.
5. The **price of oil** went **up 6%**.

聽聽看 8

1. I would like to **make** the **following proposal**.
2. We should **increase** our **prices** by **3%**.
3. This **supplier** is **charging too much**.

4. The customers are all asking for discounts.

5. Market share is growing, but the total market size is shrinking.

聽聽看 9

		True	False
1	George 在談論關於採購部門的事。		✔
2	業績狀況良好。		✔
3	業績在過去這一季提高了 3% 。		✔
4	消費者的支出凍結。	✔	
5	業務團隊工作很賣力。	✔	
6	業務團隊專注從既有客戶取得更大筆的訂單。		✔
7	新客戶在詢問折扣。	✔	
8	這一季的利潤會減少。	✔	

CD 內容

Track 083

I just want to say a few words about the market situation here. Unemployment has risen sharply over the last quarter. Consumer spending has slowed down recently, as people are worried about unemployment. Mortgage loans are down, and the number of houses and apartments being repossessed by the banks has risen. The volume of export has declined as shipping companies are not being granted credit notes, and insurance for credit has also declined. This has affected the exchange rate of the local currency.

【中譯】

我只想大略談一下這裡的市場情況。過去這一季以來，失業率急速攀升。由於擔心失業，最近的顧客消費力也降低。房屋抵押貸款減少，而銀行強制收回的房屋和公寓數量增加。船運公司的貸方票據不被許可，出口量也因而下滑，而且信用保險也下跌了。這些已經影響了當地貨幣的匯率。

Track 084

1. First, I'm going to talk about the background. Then, I'm going to make some proposals for dealing with the problem.
2. I'd like to look in a bit more detail at the results of the survey for each segment of the market.
3. All the respondents said they would like to own more of the product line.
4. The situation has been getting worse for a while, and if we don't take action, it will damage the company.

5. Sales rose by 20% in this period last year, but this year they have only risen by 5%. This is a very bad situation.
6. If you look here, you can see that this supplier's prices are the highest.
7. These figures suggest that the strategy has worked so far.

【中譯】

1. 首先，我會談談背景。然後，我會提出一些處理問題的建議。
2. 我想更詳細來看看每一個市場區塊的調查結果。
3. 所有的受訪者都說他們想要擁有更多該款產品。
4. 情況愈來愈糟已經持續一段時間，如果我們不採取行動，將會對公司有危害。
5. 去年同期業績提高了 20%，但今年只提高了 5%。這是很糟的情況。
6. 如果各位看這裡，你們可以看到這家供應商的價格是最高的。
7. 這些數據顯示截至目前為止這個策略是奏效的。

Track 085

1. First, I'm going to talk about the overseas markets. Then, I'm going to discuss the problems with the home market.
2. Each store in the chain did very well last year, with sales in all stores doing very well.
3. We don't have enough distributors in this market to really be able to increase our market share.
4. Costs rose by 33% last quarter because of the increase in the price of oil. This is not acceptable.
5. Here are the figures for the last quarter of last year.

【中譯】

1. 首先，我會先談談海外市場。然後，我會討論國內市場的問題。
2. 去年連鎖店的每一家店都表現得很好，每家商店的業績都表現亮眼。
3. 我們在這個市場的經銷商不夠多，無法真正提高我們的市場佔有率。
4. 由於油價上漲，上一季的成本提高了 33%。這是無法接受的。
5. 這裡是去年最後一季的數據。

Track 086

1. We are going to have to lay off at least one-third of our workforce if this recession continues.
2. We can't increase our sales with the current number of sales staff.
3. We didn't enter this market until one year ago, so that's why things are slow here.
4. The volume of trade has slowed down due to difficulties in obtaining credit.
5. Bad weather has again delayed the shipments this month.

【中譯】

1. 如果這波不景氣持續下去，我們就必須解雇至少三分之一的人力。
2. 以現有的業務員人數，我們無法提高業績。
3. 我們一年前才進入這個市場，這就是為什麼事情進展緩慢。
4. 由於信貸取得困難，貿易額已經下降。
5. 惡劣天候再度使這個月的貨運延誤。

Track 087

1. Costs have risen sharply.
2. We increased our prices.

3. The situation is very bad.

4. Market share has declined.

5. The price of oil went up 6%.

【中譯】

1. 成本大幅提高。
2. 我們提高了我們的價格。
3. 情況非常糟糕。
4. 市場佔有率已經下降。
5. 油價上漲了 6% 。

Track 088

1. I would like to make the following proposal.

2. We should increase our prices by 3%.

3. This supplier is charging too much.

4. The customers are all asking for discounts.

5. Market share is growing, but the total market size is shrinking.

【中譯】

1. 我想提出以下建議。
2. 我們應該把我們的價格提高 3% 。
3. 這家供應商索價太高了。
4. 客戶們全都在要求折扣。
5. 市場佔有率在成長，但是整體市場規模在萎縮。

Track 089

I just want to let you know what has been happening in the sales department recently. Sales are not doing so well. Sales dropped 4% in the last quarter. It's becoming more and more difficult to make sales, as most of our customers are not placing any big new orders until next year. Our sales team is working very hard and is focusing on trying to get new customers through referrals from existing customers. We've only had a limited success with this, as new machinery budgets are frozen, and new customers are asking for heavy discounts. Margins are likely to be down as well for this quarter.

【中譯】

我只想要讓各位知道最近業務部門發生了什麼事。業績的表現不盡理想，過去這一季業績下滑了4%。現在愈來愈難創造業績，因為我們大多數客戶一直到明年都不會有大筆的新訂單。我們的業務團隊非常努力，想辦法透過既有客戶的介紹，全力開發新客戶。這項努力的成果很有限，因為新機械的預算被凍結，而新客戶要求的折扣都很大。這一季的利潤很可能還是會下降。

Unit 14

All Or One?

全部還是一個？

學習重點 有沒有聽出 s，差很多！

1 Steve 針對公司現況做了一段簡報，你可以聽懂多少？請判斷下列陳述何者為 True 、何者為 False 。 Track 090

		True	False
1	公司只經營一個市場。		
2	公司只製造一種產品。		
3	公司有多種市場策略。		
4	公司經營的所有市場都表現不好。		
5	所有的產業都受到影響。		
6	公司最近只有一筆訂單。		
7	公司贏得了一些新客戶。		
8	公司必須向所有的供應商施壓。		

答案 請見 240 頁。

中文和英文最大的差異之一，就是區別單複數的方式。在英文，要表示我們所指的東西多於一個時，會在名詞字尾加上 s（或 es）。這個小小的 s 字母非常重要： customer 表示只有一個客戶； customers 就表示多於一個客戶。就我的觀察，華人在說英文時常常忽略這個 s 的發音。在本單元，就要來幫助各位提升對於名詞字尾 s 的敏感度，進而在聽簡報時能掌握正確訊息。

2 請閱讀 Steve 的簡報內容，並回答下列問題。這一次你應該更能掌握細節資訊了吧？

In the markets we operate in, our products are doing very well. The marketing strategy we have adopted has worked very well, and sales are up across the board. In the home market in particular, although the economy is not doing well, and the industry generally is suffering, our orders have increased, and we have even gained new customers. This has meant we have had to put pressure on our supplier to increase their efficiency.

Questions ：

1. 公司經營一個市場，還是更多個？你如何知道的？
2. 公司製造一種產品，還是一系列產品？你如何知道？
3. 公司採行一個行銷策略，還是更多個？你如何知道？
4. Steve 談論多個市場，還是只有一個？你如何知道？
5. 哪些產業受到影響？全部還是只有一個？你如何知道？
6. 公司有一筆大的新訂單，或是多筆小的新訂單？你如何知道？
7. 公司開發了許多新客戶，或是只有一個新的大客戶？你如何知道？
8. Steve 談的是他們所有的供應商，還是只有一個？你如何知道？

答案 請見 240 頁。

在上列敘述中，字尾是否為複數型會改變所要傳達的意思。閱讀的時候，很容易判斷是否為複數型，但用聽的時候就比較困難了一點。

讓我們來看看在商業英文中一些關鍵名詞的複數型要如何發音。大致規則為：

- 如果名詞字尾是子音，複數字尾 s 的發音是 /s/，如：market - markets。
- 如果名詞字尾是母音或 /ə/、/l/ 等有聲子音，複數字尾的發音是 /z/，如：industry - industries、file - files。

■ 如果名詞字尾的發音是 /s/ 或 /z/，複數字尾就會唸成 /sɪz/ 或 /zɪz/，如： size - sizes 。

■ 記住：這些規則適用於發音，不是拼字！

動動腦

3 請根據剛剛所學的規則，將下列名詞分類填入表格。可搭配 CD，根據單字的字尾發音來判斷，記住，要專注於聲音，不是拼字。 Track 091

■ ad 廣告
■ brand 品牌
■ client 客戶
■ company 公司
■ contract 合約
■ cost 成本
■ customer 顧客
■ decrease 減少
■ department 部門
■ economy 經濟
■ file 檔案
■ finance 財務
■ increase 增加
■ industry 產業
■ invoice 發票
■ loss 虧損
■ market 市場
■ order 訂單
■ price 價格
■ product 產品
■ sale 銷售
■ service 服務
■ size 尺寸
■ strategy 策略
■ supplier 供應商
■ target 目標
■ tax 稅

複數字尾發音為 /s/	複數字尾發音為 /z/	複數字尾發音為 /sɪz/ 或 /zɪz/

答案 請見 241 頁。核對完答案，請聽 Track 092，練習這些名詞的單、複數發音。

聽聽看

4 請聽 CD 播放的句子，並判斷 A 和 B 何者正確。

Track 093

_____ **1.** A：一個目標，多個部門。
B：多個目標，多個部門。

_____ **2.** A：一個產業，多種策略。
B：多個產業，多種策略。

_____ **3.** A：一張發票，一個檔案。
B：多張發票，多個檔案。

_____ **4.** A：多份合約，多種價格。
B：一份合約，一種價格。

_____ **5.** A：一種減少，多筆訂單。
B：多種減少，一筆訂單。

_____ **6.** A：整體財務，多筆虧損。
B：一種財務，一種虧損。

_____ **7.** A：一種稅，一家公司。
B：多種稅，多家公司。

_____ **8.** A：一則廣告，一個品牌。
B：多則廣告，多個品牌。

_____ **9.** A：一筆業績，多種成長。
B：所有業績，一種成長。

_____ **10.** A：多項成本，一家供應商。
B：一項成本，多家供應商。

_____ **11.** A：一項服務，一家客戶。
B：多項服務，多家客戶。

_____ **12.** A：一個市場，一個經濟體。
B：多個市場，多個經濟體。

_____ **13.** A：一種產品，多家客戶，一種尺寸。
B：多種產品，多家客戶，多種尺寸。

答案 請見241頁。

如果你覺得這一個練習很困難，表示你對複數字尾的敏感度還不夠，請多聽幾次。也可以回頭聽聽 Track 092，熟悉商務常用字的單數和複數發音。

聽聽看

5 現在請聽另一段簡報，並判斷下列敘述為 True 還是 False。請專注在本單元所學到的重點，看看你進步了多少。

Track 094

		True	False
1	簡報者在談論公司的財務狀況。		
2	目前的財務狀況良好。		
3	一種稅金大量增加。		
4	原物料價格已經上漲。		
5	所有的成本都已經提高。		

		True	False
6	公司在上一季的投資上有多筆虧損。		
7	主要客戶的訂單數量減少。		
8	所有部門都很努力。		

答案 請見 241 頁。

解答

聽聽看 1

		True	False
1	公司只經營一個市場。		✔
2	公司只製造一種產品。		✔
3	公司有多種市場策略。		✔
4	公司經營的所有市場都表現不好。		✔
5	所有的產業都受到影響。		✔
6	公司最近只有一筆訂單。		✔
7	公司贏得了一些新客戶。	✔	
8	公司必須向所有的供應商施壓。		✔

動動腦 2

1. 數個市場。 Steve 說的是 markets ，表示多於一個。
2. 多種產品。 Steve 說的是 products ，表示多於一種。
3. 一種策略。 Steve 說的是 strategy ，表示只有一種策略，並不是 strategies 。
4. 多個市場。 Steve 說的是 markets ，不是 market 。
5. 一種產業。 Steve 說的是 industry 。
6. 多筆小訂單。 Steve 說的是 orders ，表示有多筆訂單。
7. 許多新客戶。 Steve 說的是 customers ，表示多於一個。
8. 只有一家供應商。 Steve 談的是 supplier ，表示只有一家，並不是 suppliers 。

動動腦 3

複數字尾發音為 /s/	複數字尾發音為 /z/	複數字尾發音為 /sɪz/ 或 /zɪz/
market	ad	size
product	brand	tax
client	economy	increase
cost	strategy	decrease
contract	customer	finance
department	supplier	loss
target	order	invoice
	industry	price
	sale	service
	company	
	file	

聽聽看 4

1. B　2. A　3. B　4. A　5. A
6. A　7. B　8. B　9. B　10. A
11. B　12. B　13. B

聽聽看 5

		True	False
1	簡報者在談論公司的財務狀況。	✔	
2	目前的財務狀況良好。		✔
3	一種稅金大量增加。		✔
4	原物料價格已經上漲。	✔	
5	所有的成本都已經提高。	✔	
6	公司在上一季的投資上有多筆虧損。		✔
7	主要客戶的訂單數量減少。	✔	
8	所有部門都很努力。	✔	

CD 內容

Track 090

（英國口音）

In the markets we operate in, our products are doing very well. The marketing strategy we have adopted has worked very well, and sales are up across the board. In the home market in particular, although the economy is not doing well, and the industry generally is suffering, our orders have increased, and we have even gained new customers. This has meant we have had to put pressure on our supplier to increase their efficiency.

【中譯】

在我們所經營的市場，我們的產品表現優異。我們所採取的行銷策略非常成功，而且業績全面提升。尤其是國內市場，雖然經濟狀況不理想，這個產業一般都受到影響，我們的訂單卻增加，我們甚至贏得了新客戶。這表示我們必須向供應商施壓，讓他們提高效率。

Track 093

（英國口音）

1. The targets are set by the departments.
2. In order to stay competitive in this industry, it's important to have good strategies.
3. The invoices need to be carefully filed. The files are kept downstairs.
4. I have studied the contracts, and it seems that some of the prices were changed at the last moment.

5. We have seen a decrease in orders.
6. Our finances are not looking good at the moment. We are suffering significant losses.
7. The taxes paid by international companies are higher than local companies.
8. The ads really helped to promote the brands.
9. Sales have seen a huge increase.
10. We must try to reduce costs. Let's try to renegotiate with our supplier.
11. We are increasing the services we are able to offer to our clients.
12. The markets we operate in are very difficult at the moment. The major economies are struggling.
13. These products are among our most popular. Our customers like them because they come in different sizes.

【中譯】

1. 目標是由各部門設定。
2. 要在這個產業維持競爭力，有良好的策略很重要。
3. 發票必須仔細歸檔。檔案存放在樓下。
4. 我研究過合約，有些價格似乎在最後一刻被更動了。
5. 我們看到訂單減少。
6. 我們的財務狀況現在看起來不太好，我們蒙受重大虧損。
7. 跨國公司所付的稅比當地公司高。
8. 廣告真的有助於推廣品牌。
9. 業績有大幅成長。
10. 我們必須設法降低成本。我們試著和供應商重新協商吧。
11. 我們正在能力範圍內增加給客戶的服務。

12. 我們所經營的市場目前處境艱難，大部分地區的經濟狀況都在掙扎著求突破。

13. 這些是我們最受歡迎的產品，消費者喜歡它們，因為它們有不同尺寸。

Track 094

（英國口音）

I would like to talk briefly about our finances. Things are not looking good. We have seen increases in taxes and the prices of raw materials have also increased, affecting our costs. We saw a loss in our last quarter earnings, and a decrease in the size of orders from our main customer. We will probably not be able to meet our revenue target for the next quarter. Now, I know that all departments are working very hard to keep the company going, but things have now reached a critical stage. I'm asking for your ideas.

【中譯】

我想概略談談我們的財務狀況。情況看起來不妙，稅金增加，原物料價格也上漲，影響了我們的成本。我們看到上一季的營收處於虧損狀態，主要客戶的訂貨量減少。下一季的盈收目標很可能沒辦法達到。現階段，我知道所有部門都非常努力維持公司的運作，不過現在情況已經到了一個危急階段，我想問問各位的想法。

Unit 15

Let's Move On.

我們繼續吧。

學習重點 掌握起承轉合，就成功了一半！

聽聽看

1 Tina針對市場策略對於中國這個大市場的重要性，做了一段簡報，你可以聽懂多少？請將下列敘述按照你所聽到的先後順序編號。 Track 095

	General principles of a successful strategy
	Two case studies
	A Q&A
	A company that did not succeed
1	The importance of marketing strategies in the greater China market
	A successful company
	A description of the main features of the market

答案 請見255頁。

在最後這個單元，我們會著重在句子的重音訓練與加強各位聽細節內容的能力。想要掌握簡報的細節內容，首先要能聽出簡報的起承轉合。簡報通常有三個主要段落：

■ 簡報開場
■ 主文
■ 談論投影片上的細節

要能掌握簡報的起承轉合，你必須留意二個重點：第一，仔細聽架構性字串 (organizing set-phrase)；第二，仔細聽簡報者的語調。

我們先從簡報的開場段落開始。

在剛剛的聽力練習中，你所聽到的就是一段簡報開場範例。簡報者先說明了這場簡報的主題，即「聲明目的」 (the statement of purpose)，然後告知聽眾她將如何架構這場簡報，即「標示」 (signposting)。在這個開場中，簡報者使用了上述二種字串來呈現簡報架構。我們接著就來學習這二種字串。

說說看 **2 請研讀下列「聲明目的」和「標示」字串，並跟著 CD 練習開口說這些字串。** Track 096

聲明目的	標示
• My presentation today is going to cover ... 我今天的簡報將會涵蓋……。 • My presentation today focuses on ... 我今天的簡報會專注在……。 • Today, I'm going to talk about ... 今天我要談談……。 • This afternoon I'd like to tell you about ... 今天下午我要告訴各位關於……。 • My presentation today will deal with ... 我今天的簡報會處理關於……。	• I'm going to start with ... 我一開始會……。 • Second, I plan to discuss ... 第二，我會討論……。 • Then, I'll move on to ... 然後，我會進行到……。 • After that, we'll take a look at ... 在那之後，我們會看看……。 • To end we'll ... 最後，我們會……。

想要更熟悉這些字串的用法嗎？可以回頭聽聽 Track 095，留意這些字串如何使用。

除了字串，簡報者也使用了「四階段語調模式」來呈現簡報段落。

四階段語調模式：

1. 用下降語調結束段落。
2. 停頓。
3. 用較高聲調，使用標示字串開始另一段落。
4. 重複第一階段。

聽聽看 **3 請再聽一次 Tina 的簡報，這次請留意「四階段語調模式」。** Track 095

小叮嚀

如果你無法清楚聽出每個字串，或是不了解字串用法，藉由簡報者的停頓和語調，你還是可以掌握簡報架構。遵照「四階段語調模式」可以讓你更容易掌握簡報的起承轉合，進而聽出重要訊息，即使不是每個字都聽懂也無妨。

動動腦 **4 下列為 Track 095 的內容，請在簡報者使用「四階段語調模式」的地方畫上斜線。**

Hello everybody, and thanks for coming along. Today I'm going to talk about the importance of marketing strategies in the greater China market. I'm going to start with a description of the main features of market. Then I'll move on to look at two case studies of international companies who have invested in this market: a case of a company that implemented a very successful strategy, and a company that did not succeed. After that we'll take a look at what we can learn from these two case studies and try to arrive at some general principles for a successful marketing strategy in China. To end we'll have a Q&A.

答案 請見 255 頁。核對完答案，請練習運用四階段語調模式來唸唸這段簡報開場。

結束了簡報的開場，現在讓我們來看看簡報的中間部分，也就是主體段落。

聽聽看 **5** 請聽這段簡報的主體，並將下列敘述依照你所聽到的先後順序排列。 Track 097

	The problems of supply and logistics
	Two crucial issues
	Distribution channel
	Advertising budget

答案 請見 255 頁。

說說看 **6** 請研讀下列「架構」字串，並跟著 CD 練習它們的發音、語調。 Track 098

架構
• We need to address two crucial points here: first …, and second, … 我們在此需要談論二個重要論點：首先⋯⋯，第二⋯⋯。
• There are three main points here: first, …; second, …; and third, … 這裡有三個主要論點：首先，⋯⋯，第二⋯⋯，第三⋯⋯。

- Now, I'm going to …
  現在，我要……。
- Let's turn now to …
  我們現在接著……。
- I'd like to turn now to …
  我現在要接著……。

請再回頭聽一遍 Track 097 的簡報主體，聽的時候請留意「架構」字串在主體中如何使用，和簡報者的「四階段語調模式」。

動動腦

7 請閱讀下列 Track 097 的內容，請在簡報者使用「四階段語調模式」的地方畫上斜線 。

We need to address two crucial issues here. First, the issue of having a big enough advertising budget. We've seen how important advertising is in this market, and what happens when you don't do enough advertising. And second, the problem of distribution. Finding a reliable local distribution channel is the key to high sales. I'd like to turn now to the problems of supply and logistics.

答案 請見 256 頁。核對完答案，請練習運用「四階段語調模式」把這段簡報大聲唸出來。

接著我們來學習如何談論投影片的內容。

聽聽看

8 請聽簡報者談論這張投影片，並將下列敘述依照你所聽到的先後順序排列。 Track 099

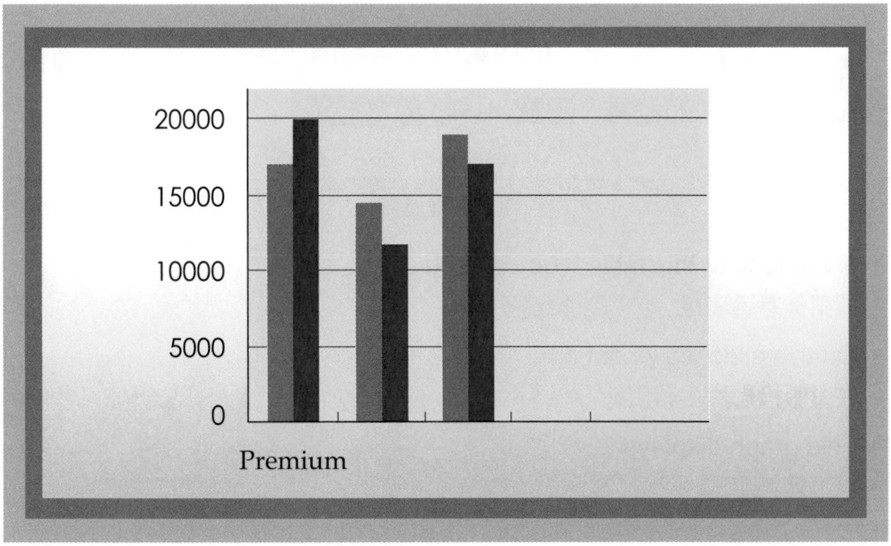

	Detailed analysis of the figures
	Increase in the Premium brand
	Costs and margins for three products
	Successful strategy

答案 請見256頁。

當簡報者在談論投影片內容時，通常會從一般資訊開始。然後請聽眾把焦點放在投影片上需要進一步說明的部分，並開始說明。接著再進行下一張投影片。所以你必須聽出四個重點：

1. 投影片上的一般資訊。
2. 投影片上的重要資訊。

3. 爲什麼這個資訊很重要。

4. 進行下一張投影片。

說說看

9 請研讀以上四個步驟所須使用的字串，並跟著 CD 練習它們的發音、語調。 Track 100

1. 一般資訊

- If you look at this table, you can see …
  如果你看這表格，你可以看到……。
- On this slide we've got …
  在這張投影片，我們有……。
- This graph displays …
  這張圖顯示出……。

2. 重要訊息

- I'd like to draw your attention to the fact that …
  我想請各位注意……。
- Look at the way that …
  看看……的方式。
- Notice how …
  注意……如何……。

3. 說明

- These figures suggest that …
  這些數據說明了……。
- These statistics show that …
  這些統計顯示……。
- It is clear from the general movement that …
  一般趨勢很清楚顯示出……。

4. 往下進行
• Moving on to the next slide. 進行下一張投影片。 • Let's turn to the next slide. 我們接著看下一張投影片。 • Now let's look at … 現在我們來看看……。

可以再回頭聽聽 Track 099，聽的時候留意上述字串的用法和簡報者的語調模式。

動動腦 **10 請閱讀 Track 099 的內容，請在簡報者使用「四階段語調模式」的地方畫上斜線 。**

If you look at this table, you can see costs and margins for the three main product lines we've had on the market during the last year. I'd like to draw your attention to the fact that there was a consistent increase in the Premium brand, while the other two key brands declined. It is clear from the general movement that the strategy the agency used for the Premium brand was a more successful strategy than the other two. Moving on to the next slide, we can analyze these figures in more detail.

答案 請見256頁。

聽聽看

11 **Kelvin** 針對學好英文的優點做了一段簡報，請將下列敘述依照你所聽到的先後順序排列。聽的時候，請專注在本單元所學到的重點，看看你進步了多少。 Track 101

	Opening
	The advantages of speaking good English
	Key service providers
1	Reasons that learning English is good for your career
	The many ways of achieving good English skills
	Body
	Three ways of learning English
	Self study
	Private teacher
	Buxiban class
	Talking about Slides
	Table of English off-site consultancies
	Classes for business English are more expensive
	Business English teachers are more experienced and better trained
	Prices and lesson types of *buxibans* providing business English

答案 請見256頁。

解答

聽聽看 1

6	General principles of a successful strategy
3	Two case studies
7	A Q&A
5	A company that did not succeed
1	The importance of marketing strategies in the greater China market
4	A successful company
2	A description of the main features of the market

動動腦 4

Hello everybody, and thanks for coming along. / Today I'm going to talk about the importance of marketing strategies in the greater China market. / I'm going to start with a description of the main features of market. / Then I'll move on to look at two case studies of international companies who have invested in this market: a case of a company that implemented a very successful strategy, and a company that did not succeed. / After that we'll take a look at what we can learn from these two case studies and try to arrive at some general principles for a successful marketing strategy in China. / To end we'll have a Q&A. /

聽聽看 5

4	The problems of supply and logistics
1	Two crucial issues
3	Distribution channel
2	Advertising budget

動動腦 7

We need to address two crucial issues here. / First, the issue of having a big enough advertising budget. We've seen how important advertising is in this market, and what happens when you don't do enough advertising. / And second, the problem of distribution. Finding a reliable local distribution channel is the key to high sales. / I'd like to turn now to the problems of supply and logistics. /

聽聽看 8

4	Detailed analysis of the figures
2	Increase in the Premium brand
1	Costs and margins for three products
3	Successful strategy

動動腦 10

If you look at this table, you can see costs and margins for the three main product lines we've had on the market during the last year. / I'd like to draw your attention to the fact that there was a consistent increase in the Premium brand, while the other two key brands declined. / It is clear from the general movement that the strategy the agency used for the Premium brand was a more successful strategy than the other two. / Moving on to the next slide, we can analyze these figures in more detail. /

聽聽看 11

	Opening
2	The advantages of speaking good English
4	Key service providers

1	Reasons that learning English is good for your career
3	The many ways of achieving good English skills
Body	
1	Three ways of learning English
4	Self study
2	Private teacher
3	*Buxiban* class
Talking about Slides	
4	Table of English off-site consultancies
2	Classes for business English are more expensive
3	Business English teachers are more experienced and better trained
1	Prices and lesson types of *buxibans* providing business English

CD 內容

Track 095

Hello everybody, and thanks for coming along. Today I'm going to talk about the importance of marketing strategies in the greater China market. I'm going to start with a description of the main features of the market. Then I'll move on to look at two case studies of international companies who have invested in this market: a case of a company that implemented a very successful strategy, and a company that did not succeed. After that we'll take a look at what we can learn from these two case studies and try to arrive at some general principles of a successful marketing strategy in China. To end we'll have a Q&A.

【中譯】

哈囉，各位，謝謝你們的蒞臨。今天我要來談談行銷策略在中國這個更廣大的市場中的重要性。一開始我會說明該市場的主要特色，然後我會繼續談論兩個在該市場投資的跨國公司的實例研究：案例一是一家公司採行一個非常成功的策略，另一家公司則並未成功。在那之後，我們再來看看從這二個實例研究我們能學到哪些事情，並試著歸納出在中國市場中成功行銷策略的一些基本原則。最後我們會有一段問答時間。

Track 097

We need to address two crucial issues here. First, the issue of having a big enough advertising budget. We've seen how important advertising is in this market, and what happens when you don't do enough advertising. And second, the problem of distribution. Finding a reliable local distribution channel is the key to high sales. I'd like to turn now to the problems of supply and logistics.

【中譯】

我們在此必須談談兩個重要議題。第一，廣告預算金額要夠大的議題。我們已經看到在這個市場上廣告有多麼重要，以及廣告不足所會發生的後果。還有第二，經銷的問題。找到一個可信賴的當地經銷管道是高業績的關鍵。現在我想接著談論供應和物流的問題。

Track 099

If you look at this table, you can see costs and margins for the three main product lines we've had on the market during the last year. I'd like to draw your attention to the fact that there was a consistent increase in the Premium brand, while the other two key brands declined. It is clear from the general movement that the strategy the agency used for the Premium brand was a more successful strategy than the other two. Moving on to the next slide, we can analyze these figures in more detail.

【中譯】

如果各位看這張表格，你們可以看到我們去年上市的三款主要產品的成本和利潤。我想請各位注意，Premium 品牌一直持續在上升，而其他兩個重要品牌卻是下降的。這個整體趨勢清楚顯示出，代理商針對 Premium 品牌採行的策略相較於其他兩個品牌是一個比較成功的策略。繼續來看下一張投影片，我們進一步來分析這些數據。

Track 101

My presentation today is going to cover the reasons that learning English is beneficial to you. I'm going to start with a brief overview of the advantages you can enjoy if you speak good English. Second, I plan to discuss the many ways you can achieve your goal of good English. After that, we'll take a look at some of the key service providers in the market. To end we'll have a Q&A. ...

【中譯】

我今天的簡報會涵蓋學習英文對各位有益的理由。一開始我會先簡單概述，如果你能說一口好英文會有哪些優點。其次，我會討論達到良好英語目標的諸多方法。在那之後，我們會來看看市場上一些提供此類服務的主要單位。最後我們會有一段問答時間。……

... and higher salaries. I'd like to turn now to the ways you can use to learn English. There are three main points here. First, you can find a private teacher. This is the most expensive, but probably the most beneficial in terms of cost effectiveness. Second, you can attend a class at a *buxiban*. This has the advantage of being much cheaper, but the class may not meet your needs exactly. And third, you can study on your own using self-study materials. However, this takes a lot of discipline. ...

【中譯】

……和更高的薪資。我現在想接著談談各位可以學英文的方式。這裡有三個重點。第一，你可以找私人家教。這是最昂貴、但從成本效益來看卻可能是收益最大的。第二，可以去補習班上課。優點是便宜許多，不過課程也許不能完全符合你的需求。還有第三，你可以利用自學素材自己學。不過，這必須有很強的自制力。……

... some data from *buxibans*. On this slide we've got the prices and lesson types of the main *buxibans* who provide business English classes. I'd like to draw your attention to the fact that classes for business English are usually more expensive than classes for general English. These statistics show that business English is more of a specialized skill requiring a more experienced and specially trained teacher. Now let's look at a comparable table for English off-site consultancies. ...

【中譯】

……從補習班得到的一些數據。在這張投影片，我們有提供商業英文課程的主要補習班的價格和課程類型。我想請各位注意，商業英文的課程通常比一般英文的課程昂貴。這些統計顯示出，商業英文是一種比較專業的技能，需要更多經驗和受過特別訓練的老師。我們現在來看看英文遠距學習顧問公司的比較表格。

NOTES

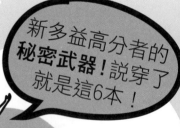

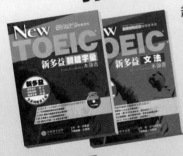

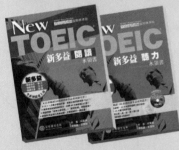

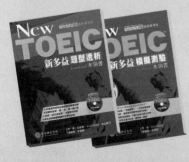